Effie Starr Zook Has One More Question

MARTHA FREEMAN

A Paula Wiseman Book

Simon & Schuster Books for Young Readers

NEW YORK   LONDON   TORONTO   SYDNEY   NEW DELHI

SIMON & SCHUSTER BOOKS FOR YOUNG READERS
An imprint of Simon & Schuster Children's Publishing Division
1230 Avenue of the Americas, New York, New York 10020

SIMON & SCHUSTER BOOKS FOR YOUNG READERS
is a trademark of Simon & Schuster, Inc.
For information about special discounts for bulk purchases, please contact Simon & Schuster Special Sales at 1-866-506-1949 or business@simonandschuster.com.
The Simon & Schuster Speakers Bureau can bring authors to your live event.
For more information or to book an event, contact the Simon & Schuster Speakers Bureau at 1-866-248-3049 or visit our website at www.simonspeakers.com.
Jacket design by Chloë Foglia
Interior design by Hilary Zarycky
The text for this book was set in Life LT Std.
Manufactured in the United States of America 0217 FFG
First Edition
2 4 6 8 10 9 7 5 3 1
Library of Congress Cataloging-in-Publication Data
Names: Freeman, Martha, 1956- author.
Title: Effie Starr Zook has one more question / by Martha Freeman.
Description: First edition. | New York : Simon & Schuster Books for Young Readers, [2017] | "A Paula Wiseman Book." | Summary: "City girl Effie Starr Zook is not excited about spending the summer on her aunt and uncle's farm in Nowheresville, Pennsylvania, until she stumbles across a mystery that leads her smack into an old family feud."—Provided by publisher.
Identifiers: LCCN 2016010813| ISBN 9781481472647 (hardback) | ISBN 9781481472661 (e-book)
Subjects: | CYAC: Mystery and detective stories. | Families—Fiction. | Pennsylvania—Fiction. | BISAC: JUVENILE FICTION / Family / General (see also headings under Social Issues). | JUVENILE FICTION / Lifestyles / Farm & Ranch Life. | JUVENILE FICTION / Mysteries & Detective Stories.
Classification: LCC PZ7.F87496 Ef 2017 | DDC [Fic]—dc23
LC record available at https://lccn.loc.gov/2016010813

For reporters who, like Effie, ask questions
in pursuit of the truth.

CHAPTER

1

Effie Starr Zook looked out the bedroom window, and what she saw made her heart go *thud*. There in the pen with Alfred the Goat stood a little boy.

Alfred the Goat was big and black with a devilish beard, a devilish temperament, and devilish big horns, too. So far, busy at his hayrack, he hadn't noticed he had company. When he did, there would be trouble.

This happened on a Thursday afternoon in June. Effie was spending the summer with her aunt and uncle. She had been there only since Sunday, but already she knew all about Alfred the Goat. One time he had knocked Uncle Ted flat in a dispute over hay. Another time Aunt Clare had been cleaning his hooves when he twisted free, turned around, and butted her. Aunt Clare said the bruise lasted for weeks. She wouldn't say where the bruise was.

Effie's bedroom window was in the back of her aunt and uncle's pretty yellow farmhouse. The window overlooked the goat pen, the brick-red barn, a grassy field, and the woods beyond. *I bet that little boy will be fine,* she thought. *I bet I can just go back to reading my book. Anyway, it's not my fault if little kids go climbing into pens with goats. Little kids are not my responsibility.*

This last sentence was barely formed when Alfred the Goat swung his head around, noticed the intruder, and raised his horns.

Effie thought, *This is not good.*

Then she closed her book and ran downstairs.

Effie Starr Zook had lived her whole life in New York City. She knew in what year the French gave Lady Liberty to America. She knew a smoothie from a lassi, a cemita from a torta, and a latte from a cappuccino. She knew where to catch the jitney for the Hamptons.

She did not know much about goats.

As she fiddled with the latch on the gate to Alfred's pen, she reassured herself: *Things usually turn out fine. Soon I'll be back to my book.*

But when the latch gave way, her knees turned watery. At the same time, a voice rang out in the distance: "Scaredy-cat! Scaredy-cat! Scaredy-scaredy-scaredy-*cat!*"

Effie looked and saw a second boy across the field, a boy about her own age. He was looking at the little one, who now stood in the opposite corner of the pen. He didn't seem to see Effie at all. *Maybe that's the big brother,* Effie thought, *and the big brother has dared the little one to climb in with Alfred the Goat and do something. But what?*

This question was soon answered. The little boy took three giant steps, reached forward, tugged the goat's pointy black beard, then turned and ran like crazy.

Alfred was surprised but hesitated only a second before putting his head down to charge. He moved fast, but Effie moved faster. She leaped and landed squarely between the advancing goat and the retreating boy.

Elsewhere at that same moment other things were happening.

In the nearby town of Penn Creek, the owner of the bookstore took a sip of coffee and started a new chapter of *Anna Karenina*. In the state capital eighty miles away, a newspaper reporter tapped her pencil, waiting for her editor to say she could have extra time to work on a big story. Across two oceans, Effie Starr Zook's pioneering aviator parents haggled with a taxi driver over the fare to a remote desert airfield.

And the Earth spun and the universe expanded, and Effie Zook braced herself. She had never been butted by a goat before. She had no idea what it would be like.

2

Alfred was a goat of few talents, but one of them was knocking things over. He had been doing it his whole life. He was good at it. But the sudden appearance of this girl messed with both his aim and his momentum. He didn't knock her over, only bumped her hard in the leg.

"Ouch!" she said at the same time the boy climbed over the fence.

Rubbing her thigh, Effie backed away from Alfred. "Ni-i-i-ice goat," she lied. "What do you say I bring you oats and you leave me alone? Isn't that a good idea?"

Alfred the Goat thought this over, but only for

a moment. He was annoyed. He wanted to do some damage. Once again, he lowered his head and readied himself to charge.

Maybe things will not be okay, thought Effie, backing up, but at the same time something shot over the fence and—*thwack*—struck the big goat in the flank. Alfred bleated and spun around. Effie grabbed her chance and, a moment later, backed through the gate to safety.

"Who are you?" the big kid asked. He had run across the field by this time. He was only a few feet away.

Effie turned to face him. He was skinny and dressed in worn denim overalls and a too-big Steelers ball cap that came down over his black eyebrows. "Did you throw a rock?" she wanted to know. She was thinking the kid must have a good arm.

"God never made a rock that could hurt that goat," the boy said. "So who are you?"

"This is my family's property," said Effie. "Who are *you*?"

The little boy, also wearing overalls, had gone to stand close to his brother. Now he took his thumb out of his mouth and said, "It isn't your property. It's Zooks'."

"I am a Zook," said Effie.

The little boy shook his head. "No, you're not. Zooks is grown-ups."

"Not all of 'em. I'm Effie Starr Zook. What was he doing in the goat pen anyway?" she asked the big boy. "Did you send him in there?"

Instead of answering the question, the big boy said, "Look, to tell you the truth, we shouldn't even be talking to you."

Effie made a face. "Well, that's preposterous. We're neighbors. Besides which, I'm a kid. I'm not dangerous."

"Maybe not," said the boy, "and maybe so."

Effie thought, *It's too bad this boy is peculiar because he's the only kid I know in the whole state of Pennsylvania.*

Effie said, "Yeah, okay, whatever. Anyway, keep your brother out of our goat pen from now on, please. Alfred's mean, in case you didn't know."

The little boy removed his thumb from his mouth again and stuck out his chin like a tough guy. "Who made you the boss of us?" he snarled.

This was so silly and unexpected that it made Effie laugh, and the big brother, too. As for the little guy, he was so embarrassed, he started to cry.

Effie felt bad. "Oh gosh. I'm sorry. Do you want a tissue? Do you want some water?"

The big boy did not feel bad. "Cut it out, E.J.," he said. "We're going home."

The little boy sniffed that he wanted a tissue, and Effie ran to the house, grabbed a handful, and came back. The little boy took one, wiped his whole face, and asked for a glass of water.

The big brother was exasperated. "Come on, E.J.," he said. "We'll get a drink at home."

Effie ignored this and gestured toward the house. "There's juice if you want," she said.

"Berry juice?" said the little boy. "That's my favorite."

3

Effie told the big boy that he could come in too.

The big boy shook his head. "My pa would skin me," he said.

"That's gross," Effie said, and closed the door.

While Effie fixed juice for the boy, she made conversation. "So, your name's, uh . . . E.J.? I mean, you don't have to tell me, not if you'll get in trouble."

"I can do what I want." The little boy took the glass of juice and guzzled half. "My name is Ezekiel Joseph. Ezekiel was a Hebrew prophet, and Joseph was married to Mary. Do you know who Mary was?"

"Jesus's mom," said Effie. "What's your brother's name?"

"I got two," E.J. said. "One's Adam, one's Luke. They're old. Do you want to hear their middle names?"

"I'd probably forget," Effie said.

"Will you forget *me*?" E.J. asked.

"I probably won't," said Effie.

"Promise you won't," said the boy, and Effie promised. . . . At the same moment someone knocked on the back door. When Effie opened it, there was the kid in the Steelers cap. It was his turn to look embarrassed.

"May I have E.J. back, please?" he said, and then the words poured out. "Look, I'm sorry. I know I shouldn't've dared him to pull that old goat's beard, but he drives me crazy sometimes—the way he's so stuck-up and sure of himself. All the boys in my family are that way. Then he won't do what I want when I'm minding him. He told me nothing scared him, and I said what about the Zooks' goat . . . and it kind of went from there."

"He might've really been hurt," Effie said.

"May I have him back?" the kid said.

"Come on, E.J.," Effie called. "Your brother's here. Time to go home."

E.J. appeared in the doorway between the kitchen and the mudroom. "That's not my brother," he said.

"Oh!" said Effie. "I'm sorry. I just assumed he—"

But before Effie could say what she assumed, the big kid laughed—more of a giggle—and tugged at the Steelers cap, which fell to the ground, revealing a whole lot of wavy dark hair.

"I'm his sister," the kid said, "and my name is Moriah Yoder. And, like you guessed, we live on the other side of the woods. But please don't tell my pa I said so."

"I don't know your pa," said Effie, "and I'm sorry I thought you were a boy."

Moriah shrugged. "Doesn't matter. According to Mama, I don't have a lady shape yet, which is lucky for me, says Mama. E.J., we have weeding to do. They'll be looking for us."

"You're welcome to come over anytime," said Effie. "I don't know other kids around here."

"Thanks," said Moriah, "but I don't think your relatives will be mailing us invitations. We wouldn't be here now, only I saw the truck was gone. I never counted on you."

Effie was baffled. "I don't understand."

"Me neither," said Moriah. "All I know is something happened a long time ago, and it's grown-up stuff."

Moriah put her hand on E.J.'s shoulder and steered him toward home. Wriggling out of her grasp, he said, "Thank you for the juice, Effie Starr Zook!"

"You're welcome," said Effie, and she watched them walk across the field. Halfway home, Moriah waved a final time and called, "Good-bye!"

"Good-bye, Moriah!" Effie raised her hand back. She was hoping Moriah might look around, but she didn't.

4

When Moriah and E.J. disappeared into the trees, Effie felt a pang as if she'd lost a friend.

She told herself she was being preposterous. *You don't even know that girl! Also, she was peculiar. Why wouldn't she come in the house? Why wasn't she even supposed to talk to me?*

Effie thought it was possible that Moriah might be Amish. E.J. had said his name was from the Bible, and Effie knew the Amish were very religious. Effie had seen Amish people selling vegetables and baked goods at outdoor markets by the road. She had seen their black carriages lit by lanterns at night and pulled by trotting horses.

She tried to think of what else she knew about the Amish. They mostly kept to themselves. They didn't use electricity. They didn't drive cars. They had their own language and their own schools.

But Amish girls had to wear dresses all the time, didn't they? Not overalls and Steelers caps.

Still puzzling, Effie went to make sure Alfred the Goat was okay. Back at his hayrack, he lifted his head when Effie looked over the fence at him.

Until she'd gotten to her aunt and uncle's farm, Effie had always thought goats were cute. Then she'd taken a good look at Alfred's eyes. A goat's pupils are horizontal oblongs on the iris—very weird. Uncle Ted had explained that the shape and placement helped goats see threats to the far left or far right.

"It's nature's way of helping a poor defenseless goat spot a predator," he'd said.

Defenseless? Effie could feel the spot where Alfred's horns had bumped her. *If you ask me, those eyes are signs of a deep-down character flaw,* she thought. *You just can't trust a goat.*

Out loud, Effie said, "You know it wasn't me that

threw the rock, right?" She worried Alfred might want revenge.

The goat's answer was to raise his tail and release a pile of pellets.

"Gross," said Effie, but she was also relieved. Apparently the rock hadn't damaged the parts in charge of digestion.

Effie was still standing by Alfred's pen when she heard her aunt and uncle's truck coming up the driveway. Boris, the old, furry, filthy farm dog, had been napping on the porch. Now he roused himself and barked once by way of greeting.

If you were any kind of watchdog, you would've defended Alfred from invaders, Effie thought. But she wasn't surprised that Boris had slept through the whole episode. Her aunt and uncle said he heard only things he didn't expect would cause him any trouble.

The driveway from the road to the house was long, and several minutes passed before the red pickup pulled up beside Effie, and Uncle Ted jumped out.

"Greetings, sprite!" he said. "Did you miss us? Do you want to help us unload?"

"You don't have to," said Aunt Clare. "It's hot, dusty work. You might not like it."

Effie said she didn't mind, and her uncle passed her a white plastic sack of feed from the bed of the truck. It was almost as big as she was.

Effie wanted to ask her aunt and uncle about Moriah and E.J., but the two of them were talking to each other. Effie heard words like *deed* and *title* and *parcel*.

What could possibly be more boring?

Finally there was a break in the conversation, and Effie jumped in. "You know the kids that live on the other side of the woods?" she said.

Aunt Clare and Uncle Ted stopped what they were doing and looked first at her and then at each other.

"What?" said Effie.

"Oh dear," said Aunt Clare.

Uncle Ted's smile looked forced. "I have an idea, sprite. We'll talk about it later. Are you free for hors d'oeuvres? There will be cheese, crackers, dips, and ginger ale—with a cherry if you want one. Meanwhile, isn't that bag too heavy for you?"

"It's fine," said Effie, but her uncle already had

jumped down from the truck bed and taken it out of her arms.

"Your mother would never forgive me if you strained anything," said her aunt. "Don't you have a book to read or something to watch on that tablet thing of yours?"

Effie said, "I guess," and turned back toward the house. Going up the steps to the porch, she happened to glance down. There among the seedlings in the flower bed lay a black-and-gold Steelers ball cap.

CHAPTER

5

Effie's Aunt Clare was beautiful. Effie's mother was beautiful. Effie's father and uncle were, to put it plainly, hunks.

Any of them could've been a model or a movie star, according to Jasmine, Effie's best friend at home in New York City. Effie had learned not to mind when she heard that kind of comment, even though it implied astonishment that someone as ordinary-looking as Effie could be the near relation of gorgeous.

And Effie *was* ordinary-looking. Among the other eleven-year-old girls at her school, she was a little shorter than average and a little more square. Her hair was brown and opinionated. Her best feature, her eyes, were warm and brown besides being unusually large like her mother's and aunt's.

It was obvious to everyone in the family, including Effie, where her looks came from. Except for the wide eyes, she was the spitting image of her great-grandmother, whose name had also been Effie. The first Effie had died before the second one was born, but there was a black-and-white photograph of her in a silver frame that hung on the wall by Effie's mother's desk. There were photos of Effie's great-grandfather all over the place—with celebrities, with generals, with politicians—but there was only the one photo of his wife.

Effie was looking at this photo one day while her mother worked at the computer. "Why does she look so sad?" Effie asked.

"She doesn't look sad," said Effie's mother, whose name was Molly.

Effie took a step closer. The photograph showed only Effie the First's head and shoulders. She had round cheeks and a short nose. Her glossy black hair was parted in the middle and pulled back. She was wearing a light-colored blouse that tied in front. She was a grown-up but not yet old, maybe the age of Effie's mom now.

"She does too look sad," Effie insisted. "Why?"

This happened on a Saturday afternoon two months before Effie went to stay with her aunt and uncle. Truthfully, Effie's mom wasn't paying much attention to the conversation. Her mind was on the picture of an airplane wing on the computer screen in front of her. The wing belonged to *Sunspot I,* which she and Effie's dad were going to fly around the world.

"What?" said her mom. "I don't know. She was very kind. That's why we named you after her. She loved your aunt and me. Maybe that was because she didn't have daughters of her own, only a son."

"Her son was Grandpa Bob," Effie said. "Now he's dead too. He moved to Florida and got too much sun and too many seafood platters."

Effie's mom didn't look up. "Uh-huh," she said.

"And the first Effie was married to Great-Grandpa Gus. He's the reason we're rich. He's the one that invented the barf bag."

Molly corrected her daughter automatically. "We are not rich," she said. "We are well fixed. And it's not a barf bag. It's an emesis bag. And Gus Zook invented many, many other things too. He was a great man."

This was how it went in Effie's family. You never said "rich." You never said "barf bag." You never mentioned Gus Zook without adding, "He was a great man."

Effie knew this by heart, but she was annoyed that her mother was ignoring her. "Right," she said, "and the definition of 'emesis' is 'barf.'"

"*Effie?*" Her mother swiveled her chair around. "Sweetheart, do we have to have this conversation now? Your dad and I have a lot to do before we leave."

"I know," said Effie.

"I love you," her mom added.

"I know," said Effie. But she was too annoyed to say "I love you" back.

Effie had begged to be allowed to go with her parents on their round-the-world trip. She knew she wouldn't get to fly in *Sunspot I* herself. There was no room for passengers. There was only one seat for one pilot at a time. Her parents were going to trade off flying.

Effie had offered to help out. She could wash the windshield or vacuum the cockpit. The plane was powered by special solar batteries, and she could change them. She could even carry the bags.

Effie usually got her way. But for once her parents were firm.

"Too dangerous," her father had told her.

Effie had frowned. "I don't like the sound of that," she said. "If it's dangerous for me, it's dangerous for you."

"No need to worry about us, sweetheart," her mom had said. "We're grown-ups. We can take care of ourselves."

"That's illogical," Effie had said. "There are plenty of grown-ups who can't take care of themselves. You would know this if you watched more TV."

"Your father and I are not *those* grown-ups," said her mother.

Even with logic on her side, Effie could see there was no point in arguing further. So it was decided that while her parents were gone, she would stay at Zook Farm.

A long time before, Zook Farm had belonged to

Gus and the first Effie. Grandpa Bob had not been interested in living there, so the house had sat vacant till Aunt Clare and Uncle Ted moved in. They raised vegetables, not goats. Alfred the Goat was the last descendant of the herd that had belonged to Effie's great-grandmother, Effie the first.

In late May, Effie's dad left for the Arabian Peninsula, where the flight of *Sunspot I* would begin. He would do last-minute preparations on the ground. Later, Effie's mom would join him.

But first she helped pack up what her daughter needed for the summer in the family Land Rover and drove her to Pennsylvania. They had just crossed the Delaware River when Mom mentioned that Aunt Clare and Uncle Ted didn't know much about kids.

"Are you saying they don't want me?" Effie asked. "Because now is a bad time to bring that up."

"No, no, no," her mother said. "Your aunt and uncle love you. It's just that they don't have kids of their own, and they aren't around kids much. But I told them you are very self-sufficient. 'You won't have to worry about her for one minute,' I told them. 'She is bringing books and her iPad. She will be fine.'"

For a few minutes after that the only sounds in the car were the whoosh and hum of the road.

"Do you like your sister?" Effie asked. Not having a sibling of her own, Effie was more-than-average interested in how that whole thing worked.

"Of course," Mom said. "I love her."

"But do you like her?" Effie repeated.

"Of course," Mom said again. "Well . . . we are very different. I'm the big sister and I've always been more, I guess you'd say, outgoing. You won't find Clare designing a solar airplane, for example, or flying one either. She's too much of a worrier for one thing, and for another she never had much drive." It was quiet for a moment before Mom added, "Not that that's a bad thing. It takes all kinds to make up a world."

"Or a family," Effie said.

"Yes," said her mom. "Or a family."

"I want a bicycle," Effie said. "I want a bicycle so I can go places without bothering Aunt Clare and Uncle Ted. A bicycle will make me more self-sufficient."

"Hmmm," said her mother. "Do you suppose it's

safe for you to ride a bike around Penn Creek?"

Effie shrugged. "According to you, in Penn Creek, nothing ever happens."

Eyes fixed on the road, Effie's mother nodded. "That's true," she said. "Let's stop and get you a bike."

Effie used her phone to find the nearest bike store, and a few minutes later they pulled off Highway 80. When they resumed their trip, a blue fifteen-speed bike hung from a new black bike rack on the back of the Land Rover.

"Thank you," Effie said.

"Just promise you'll wear your helmet," her mom said.

Effie had promised, and now—with that in mind—she retrieved the helmet, which was purple and silver, from its hook in the mudroom. She hadn't actually worn it yet or gotten her bike out of the garage either.

Maybe, she thought, *this will be the start of an adventure of my own.*

6

I'm going for a bike ride—okay?" Effie called across the yard to Aunt Clare, who was kneeling among the annuals, pulling weeds.

"What's in the backpack?" Aunt Clare asked.

Effie said, "Nothing." Then she realized that sounded lame. "I mean, uh . . . I'm returning something to a friend."

"That's nice. Have fun," Aunt Clare replied, and she blew Effie a kiss.

The morning after Effie arrived, Aunt Clare and Uncle Ted had given her what they called the grand tour. Across the fence from the flower garden were lettuce, cucumbers, and scallions, all of them almost ready for harvest. Behind the barn were strawberry plants just leafing out, and tomatoes, too, transplanted from the greenhouse. This early in the season, the strawberries themselves were just hard green buds and the tomatoes only yellow flowers on sticky vines. In August there would be zucchini, peppers, and leeks. In the fall there would be pumpkins and potatoes.

Aunt Clare and Uncle Ted had told Effie she was free to wander and explore wherever she wanted. There was only one place to avoid—the old shed at the far end of the driveway. There was nothing interesting in it or secret, either, but it had been used for storage so long that it was crammed to the rafters with junk.

"You wouldn't want a pile of heavy, dusty something to topple onto your head, sprite," her uncle had said.

"Not to mention there are probably rats and possums and snakes in there," her aunt had said.

Effie had promised to stay out.

Now she fastened the strap on her flashy new helmet, rolled the bike onto the driveway, threw her leg over the seat, and nudged herself forward with her toe.

Hey—I'm moving! Look at me! she thought just as the left pedal hit her left foot and the bike stopped, teetered, tipped, and fell—bringing Effie down too.

Lying on the ground, Effie thought, *This is not good.* On the other hand, she wasn't dead and— equally important—no one had seen her fall.

Effie really could ride a bicycle. She and Jasmine had learned out on the island one summer. Unfortunately, she had never had much chance to practice. This summer she was determined to get better.

So she disentangled herself from the bike, stood up, and wheeled it to the highest point on the driveway. North, south, east, west, all she saw was green— corn shoots, soybeans, and alfalfa in the neighbors' fields; grass on the hillsides; the clean, bright leaves of the trees. Over the ridgetop beyond the road, birds flew in silhouette against the blue sky. She saw spotted cows in a field down the road. She did not see any people.

Wondering if she'd ever get used to such a lonesome view, Effie threw her leg over the seat again, pushed off, and this time kept her balance, soon gaining speed. At the bottom of the driveway was the winding two-lane road that led to town. Without stopping, Effie stood up to look both ways, saw that the road was clear, crossed, turned left, and pushed down on the pedals hard.

7

Only one vehicle passed Effie on the road, but it was a doozy, a truck hauling chickens that bore down with a roar, spraying road grit and feathers in its wake. Effie looked straight ahead, clutched the handlebars, and kept going, reaching Moriah's driveway soon after.

The driveway was marked by a battered black mailbox atop a post. YODER was written on the box in red paint. Effie looked around for cars, then crossed the road and started up the hill. She could feel her thigh muscles turning to spaghetti and the ache of the bruises on her legs.

Effie caught her breath when the driveway leveled

out and then looked up. In front of her sprawled a one-story house with a tiny lawn and beds of faded, sickly pansies by the front door. Air conditioners protruded from some of the windows. A blue car was parked by the garage.

Electricity and cars, Effie thought, *so I guess they're not Amish. But maybe they're poor?*

Even if Effie's own parents never let her say "rich," that was what they were. They lived in a big house with a view of the Brooklyn Bridge. Besides the usual rooms, it had a gym for exercising and a theater for movies. Neither her mom nor her dad had to work at a regular job. They were well fixed, they told her, and because of that they could do things like fly solar airplanes around the world.

We are lucky, they told Effie, and you are lucky too.

Thinking of E.J. and Moriah, Effie imagined herself as a princess in a fairy tale, a princess smiling down kindly on others less fortunate. She would bestow on them toys and canned goods and blankets. *It's nothing,* she would tell them.

With these pleasing thoughts in her head, she

leaned the new bike against the side of the garage, hung her helmet from the handlebars, turned, and went up the walk to the door. Before she had rung the bell, she heard a dog bark and then—*uh-oh*— here it came, a big, hound-shaped beast galloping straight for her.

I hate the country! thought Effie. *First a goat, now this!*

But instead of running her over, the dog stopped short, sat back on his haunches, and howled.

"Quiet, Fred-o! Be quiet now!" said a voice, and the front door opened to reveal a woman with blond hair and tired eyes who was dressed in pink sweats. "Well, my goodness, who are you?" she said, and then, "Are you all right, hon? You'd better come in. You're gonna need Band-Aids. Oh—and would you mind taking your shoes off? It's one of the hygiene precepts."

"What's a hygiene precept?" Effie asked. Then she looked down at herself and saw her left shin was bruised and striped with bicycle grease, her T-shirt was smudged, and a trail of dried blood snaked from her skinned elbow to her wrist.

"I guess I do look a little beat-up," she admitted, "and thank you very much for the offer, but I just came to see Moriah. I have her hat."

Effie had put the Steelers cap into her school backpack, which she now slid off her shoulders. The woman looked at the brand name and raised her eyebrows. "Hang on a second. You wouldn't by chance be a Zook?"

Effie didn't like the sound of that. "What's the matter with Zooks?"

The woman seemed to make a calculation. "Never mind your shoes," she said. "Just come on in quickly now, and be ready to leave in a hurry. Go find the paper towels in the kitchen, and I'll get Band-Aids. Once you're fixed up, you can get along home."

Effie didn't see what the hurry was. Plus now she was embarrassed about her backpack. Of course she knew it was a nice brand, but Jasmine had the exact same backpack. So did a lot of kids.

Anyway, as soon as she came into the house, she saw that this family wasn't poor at all. The living room was full of stuff—big TV, two sofas, framed photos on the wall. There was a second TV in the kitchen, along with the usual appliances, everything clean and shiny. Sadly, Effie let go of her kind princess fantasy and looked around for the paper towels. Tacked to the wall by the kitchen table was a sheet of lined notebook paper that read *Precept 47: Clean feet are happy feet.*

Effie had a lot of questions for the woman when she came back with Band-Aids and antiseptic spray. "Are you Mrs. Yoder?" she asked. "Is Moriah home? What's a hygiene precept, anyway? I'm sorry if I'm a bother. I'm staying with my aunt and uncle this summer. Do you know them? They live—"

"I know where they live," the woman said quickly. "Hold out your elbow. This might sting."

It did sting; Effie made a face.

"How come you have Moriah's hat?" the woman asked.

"I found it," Effie said without explaining further. She was annoyed that the woman asked questions but wouldn't answer them.

"Listen, hon," the woman went on. "Now that you're patched up, you better leave the hat with me and get on back to Zooks'."

"But I want to see Moriah," said Effie. She was used to getting her way and ready to argue, but before she could, she heard a noise outside—tires on gravel, a car coming.

"Horse feathers!" said the woman, suddenly flustered.

"What's the matter?" asked Effie.

"Go out the back!" the woman said. "No, wait. That won't work. He will've seen the bike. Just keep quiet, okay? And whatever you do, don't say 'Zook.' You're just any random stranger that wandered in for Band-Aids."

Effie had lived all her life in America's biggest city, and she had traveled with her parents to Europe, Machu Picchu, Hawaii, Japan, and Alaska. She had met all kinds of people and done all kinds of things. But never and nowhere had Effie had an experience as strange as this one.

She felt anxious, but also curious. What would happen next?

8

njelica? Where are ya? In the kitchen?" The man's voice was big, and so were his heavy footfalls.

Before Anjelica—so that was her name—could answer, the back door opened, and E.J. tumbled in, followed by Moriah. Busy removing their shoes, they didn't notice Effie right away.

Anjelica muttered, "Oh glory," at the same time a man came through the doorway from the living room. Like Moriah and E.J., he wore denim overalls with a T-shirt underneath. He was big all over—tall and wide without being fat. He had abundant dark blond hair on his head, but the most striking thing about him was the hair on his face—the biggest beard Effie had ever seen in real life.

"Anjelica Tiffany Yoder," he thundered, "if I've told you one time, I've told you ten thousand . . . Oh." He saw Effie and stopped in his tracks. "Excuse me, young lady. I guess the bike outside belongs to you."

"Effie-e-e!" Now E.J. noticed her too and grinned. "She's a Zook, Papa. Did you know there's Zooks that aren't grown up at all?"

The man frowned. "A Zook?"

"I'm Effie Starr Zook." Effie held out her hand. "It's nice to meet you, Mr. Yoder."

For a moment Mr. Yoder looked surprised at the very fact of Effie's hand, but then he recovered and took it in his own. "Rob Yoder," he said. "I see you've got your shoes on in the house as well. Best to come along now. I will drive you home."

"Wait!" E.J. protested. "She just got here. I wanna show her my snail shell collection. It's okay, isn't it, Mama? She's nice even if she is a Zook."

Mr. Yoder raised his eyebrows. "How does a son of mine know that this young lady is nice?"

"It's my fault, Pa," said Moriah. "Don't blame E.J."

Mr. Yoder looked at the members of his family in turn. "Seems to be some kind of rebellion afoot, one we will discuss when I come back. Miss Zook?" He turned to Effie. "Come along with me now, please."

"I've got a bike. I can ride home," Effie said.

"We'll throw that in the back of the truck." Mr. Yoder gestured. "After you."

Effie had never been bossed so much in her life. She looked to Moriah for help. When Moriah only shook her head and shrugged, Effie surrendered. She didn't want her and E.J. to get in trouble. She didn't like Mrs. Yoder looking upset. "You left this." She held the cap out, and Moriah took it.

"Mama!" E.J. protested.

"What your papa does is for the best," his mother said.

Outside, Effie had an idea. "My aunt and uncle wouldn't like me going in a truck with a stranger," she said. "I think I'd better ride home myself."

Mr. Yoder nodded. "You've got a phone, I expect? Go ahead and call them. I'll wait."

Oh, fine—still telling me what to do, Effie thought. But she pulled the phone from her pocket and texted Aunt Clare:

I'm OK. Mr. Yoder wants to give me ride home. Ok?

Effie expected a long, awkward pause, but the answer came right away.

!!!? yeh okay CU soon hurry

"Clare said yes, didn't she?" said Mr. Yoder. "See? I'm harmless."

He put the bike in the bed of the pickup, and both of them climbed in the cab. He turned the key, and the truck started up. As he drove, Mr. Yoder talked. "So, Effie Zook, are you spending the whole summer here?"

Effie said, "While my parents are away," and glanced sideways. Mr. Yoder's beard was marvelous, like a third person in the truck, almost. Did it house small birds and insects? Did he have to have it dry cleaned?

"Ah, yes, the solar airplane," Mr. Yoder said.

"How do you know about that?" Effie asked.

"Everyone knows about it," he said. "You got to remember you're in a small town now, a town your great-grandpa put on the map. Since your mom and Clare are his grandchildren, they're celebrities, and so are you."

Effie had visited her aunt and uncle before, but

only for a couple of days at a time. She'd never met anyone else who lived here. "I didn't think of that," she said.

Mr. Yoder turned right onto the two-lane road. "I see your parents gave you your dad's last name— Starr—as a middle name," he said. "And your own last name is Zook after your mom."

"My parents think girls should carry their mom's name and boys their dad's," Effie explained. "Only I don't have a brother."

Mr. Yoder shook his head. "Your parents would think that. And 'Effie,' of course, is for your great-grandma."

Effie nodded, then thought of something. "Have you lived here a long time, Mr. Yoder? Did you know my great-grandparents?"

Mr. Yoder turned right once more. The truck ascended the Zooks' long driveway. "You ask a lot of questions, don't you, Effie? But no. She died long before our family moved in. I grew up in Johnstown, but my little farm once belonged to my grandmother. I bought it back a few years ago. The story's similar to your aunt and uncle's, in fact."

Mr. Yoder pulled the truck up beside the yellow farmhouse. Aunt Clare and Uncle Ted must've been watching through a window because they came out the front door right away.

Knowing it was probably hopeless, Effie tried one last time. "Can't Moriah come over someday? Or I could come to your house when it's more convenient. I'm a good guest. Honest."

"Visits won't be possible, Effie," Mr. Yoder said. "I'm gonna get your bicycle now, and then I'll be going. You have a nice summer." He swung out of the truck, raising a hand at the same time to acknowledge Effie's aunt and uncle on the porch. Behind the beard, he might've been smiling, or not. A moment later, Effie had her bike. The last Effie saw of Moriah's dad was a red, white, and blue sticker on the truck's back bumper: BEARDS FOR AMERICA.

I wonder what that's all about, Effie thought. She had about a thousand additional questions, but her aunt spoke first.

"Are you okay? What's with all the Band-Aids? Please tell me you didn't fall off your bike on the road.

Your mother wouldn't like it if I let you do that."

"Not on the road," said Effie truthfully. "And I'm just gonna change my clothes if that's okay."

"Go right ahead," said her uncle. "And then come on back downstairs. You know what time it is, don't you, sprite? It's time for hors d'oeuvres!"

9

Effie washed in the upstairs bathroom, then changed her clothes. In her room, she noticed that the book she was reading, *Pippi Long-stocking*, still lay in the chair where she'd dropped it to go save E.J. from Alfred the Goat. It was an ancient hardcover she had found on a shelf in the bedroom. On the flyleaf was a note written by the first Effie to Aunt Clare when Aunt Clare was a little girl: *Dearest Clare, May you always be as brave as Pippi! Best love, Grandma.*

Effie had studied the note and even traced the handwriting with her finger. What had her great-grandmother been like? She was kind. She was sad.

She believed girls should be brave. Her handwriting was round and loopy.

When Effie got downstairs, her aunt and uncle were waiting for her in the parlor, which was across the entry hall from the dining room. Unlike the rest of the house, the parlor looked the same as when Effie's mom and aunt were little girls visiting their grandparents: fussy, uncomfortable furniture. Gilded mirror. Striped wallpaper. Room-sized floral rug with a gold fringe.

Uncle Ted jumped up when Effie came in. "One cherry or two, sprite?" he asked.

"Two, please," said Effie.

In the corner of the parlor was a wooden cart with an ice bucket, bottles, and glasses. Uncle Ted dropped cherries into a glass, added ice and ginger ale, then handed the drink to Effie. Effie sat down on the little couch that the grown-ups called a settee. In front of her on the coffee table was a tray with slices of cheese, crackers, olives, and salted nuts—in other words, hors d'oeuvres.

Effie hadn't realized how hungry she was till she saw them.

"Now, then, sprite." Uncle Ted grabbed a handful of nuts and sat down beside Aunt Clare. "We have put you off long enough. What is it you want to know?"

"Easy questions first, please," said Aunt Clare.

"What is Beards for America?" Effie asked.

Aunt Clare nodded and sipped her drink. "I am no authority," she said after a moment, "but I guess you would say it's a cross between a political party and a philosophy."

"A political party is like the Republicans and the Democrats," Effie said. "I've heard of them, so how come I've never heard of Beards for America?"

"It's tiny, only exists right here around Penn Creek," said Aunt Clare.

"The Facebook page has 157 likes," her uncle added.

"Is Mr. Yoder in charge?" Effie asked. "He has an amazing beard."

"I believe one of their ideas is that all men ought to grow beards." Her uncle rubbed his own hairless chin.

"What does that have to do with politics?" Effie asked.

"Your guess is as good as mine," said Aunt Clare.

"It's just one of their ideas—precepts, they call them. Maybe they think that shaving is a waste of time and water."

"I think I know another precept," said Effie, "one that goes like this: 'Clean feet are happy feet.' I saw it on a paper in the Yoders' kitchen."

"Hard to argue with keeping your feet clean," said Uncle Ted. "As for shaving, I think there might be symbolism involved. Have you ever heard of Samson and Delilah?"

"Sure," said Effie. "It's a Bible story. Samson was a strong man, a warrior long ago. Delilah was his wife. One night she cut his hair while he was asleep, and when he woke up he wasn't strong anymore. But that's a story! Nobody really believes that hair makes you strong."

"Some religions require the men to wear beards," said Aunt Clare. "The Sikhs in India, for example, and orthodox Jews. Amish men grow beards when they get married."

"I think Mr. Yoder might see beards as a symbol of strength—male strength, that is," said Uncle Ted.

"Well, then, he's a sexist," said Effie. She knew

from school that a sexist believes one gender is better than the other. It was bad to be a sexist. Thinking about that, Effie remembered how Moriah got mad at E.J. for being stuck-up and sure of himself.

"I don't know if Mr. Yoder considers himself a sexist," Uncle Ted said, "but maybe it's significant that all the BFA members I ever heard of are men."

"There's one more thing, Effie," said Aunt Clare. "It's difficult to explain, but here it is: Mr. Yoder claims that BFA was inspired by the ideas of your great-grandfather."

Effie was so surprised, she almost choked on a breadstick. "How can that be? Gus Zook was a great man. He wasn't a sexist, was he?"

"He was a great man," Aunt Clare said.

"And like Mr. Yoder, he had a great beard," said Uncle Ted.

"I've seen it in pictures," said Effie.

"But ideas can be slippery things," said Aunt Clare. "Your great-grandfather had a lot of them. I think Mr. Yoder picked the ones he liked best, then added some of his own."

"*Voilà!*" said Uncle Ted. "BFA was born."

Effie fished a cherry out of her ginger ale, put it in her mouth, and chewed it thoughtfully. "If BFA is like a political party, does Mr. Yoder want to be president?" she asked.

"I think his sights are set a little lower," said Aunt Clare. "I think he wants to be mayor of Penn Creek."

"Are you serious?" Uncle Ted raised his eyebrows.

Aunt Clare shrugged. "So says my hairdresser."

"He can't possibly win," said Uncle Ted.

"He can if no one else runs," said Aunt Clare.

"Who's the mayor now?" Effie asked.

"Nobody," said Aunt Clare. "The old one dropped dead shoveling snow last winter. The election's in November, but most people can't even be bothered to vote. I'd say Mr. Yoder has a good chance."

"Will you vote for him?" Effie asked.

"I'd rather vote for a rattlesnake," said Aunt Clare.

Effie took a breath and tried to organize her thoughts. "I don't get it. If Mr. Yoder admires Gus Zook, it means our families ought to agree on stuff. They ought to be friends. But you say Mr. Yoder's worse than a rattlesnake. And it was really weird the way they acted when I was over there, like *Zook* is a bad word or something."

"Were they mean to you?" Aunt Clare asked.

Effie shook her head. "Not mean. Just bossy. And I'm not allowed to see Moriah or go over there anymore—so that's my next question. Why not?"

"Oh dear," Aunt Clare said again. Then she shot Uncle Ted a look.

"It's difficult to explain, sprite," he said, "but what it comes down to is bad blood between our two families."

Picturing a bloody creek in the woods, Effie said, "Gross."

"'Bad blood' is a figure of speech," her uncle explained. "In other words, long ago our families disagreed, and the disagreement is still causing problems, and everybody's still mad."

Effie remembered a story from Sunday school, the one about Isaac and Ishmael. Their father was Abraham, but they had different mothers, and the mothers didn't like each other. When the boys grew up and had families of their own, the families didn't like each other either. There was bad blood between them, just like Uncle Ted was saying.

"What did our families disagree about?" Effie asked. "Are you and Aunt Clare mad? Are my parents? Am I supposed to be mad too?"

"Oh dear," said Aunt Clare.

Uncle Ted sighed. "Has anyone ever told you, Effie, that you ask a lot of questions?"

"Pretty much everyone," said Effie.

Aunt Clare jumped up. "Would you look at the time? Shall we order pizza? Alternatively, we could order pizza."

Around Penn Creek, there were only three places to eat: the diner, which closed at three in the afternoon, and two pizzerias. You had to drive to pick up the food too—no delivery service. It was nothing like Brooklyn, where Effie was used to ordering any food she wanted anytime from her phone.

Even though Effie was hungry, she had more important things than food on her mind. Was there some kind of family secret? If there was, Aunt Clare and Uncle Ted should tell her. She was part of the family. Why were the grown-ups acting so mysterious?

"Wait a second!" she protested.

But it was too late. Her aunt was pulling out her phone to dial a pizza place. Her uncle was clearing away the glasses.

"We've got all summer to talk, Effie," said Uncle Ted. "Right now I am going to set the table."

CHAPTER

10

Effie tried to Skype her parents before she turned out her light that night. Where they were, it was seven in the morning. They would be wide-awake and prepping for the big departure. The plan was for her dad to pilot *Sunspot I* first and her mother to fly on a commercial jet to meet him. At the next stop, they would trade off.

Effie got no answer on Skype, only the singsong ringtone. She gave up, but she wasn't worried. Her parents had warned her that connections might be unreliable. Still, it was a frustration. She had hoped maybe they would answer her questions about her family.

Probably it doesn't matter, she thought. *They would have said they're much too busy.*

On the wall above Effie's bed was a world map. She and her mother had hung it up just before her mother left to go back to New York. *Sunspot I*'s route was marked in orange dashes. It started and ended in Abu Dhabi on the Arabian Peninsula. In between, there were stops in India, Burma, China, Japan, Hawaii, Mexico, and Morocco.

"I'm leaving you pushpins, too," Molly had told Effie. "You can plot our progress right here"—she put her finger on one of the latitude lines—"along the twentieth parallel. That will be fun, won't it?"

Effie had thought, *Fun is the wrong word.*

Effie had said, "I guess so. Thank you."

Then her mother had pulled her close to say good-bye.

Effie was usually brave, but this was hard, and she'd had to squeeze her eyes shut to stop the tears. "Are you sure I can't go with you?" she asked, but her mouth was pressed against her mother, muffling her voice.

"What?" Her mother let go. "I didn't hear that."

Effie stepped away and sniffled. "Never mind. Have a good trip. Tell Dad I love him. Don't forget to come back."

"I promise to come back," her mom had said.

By today—Thursday—there should have been two pushpins in the map. Instead, there was only the one that marked the starting point. Her parents had been delayed by sandstorms. But Effie shouldn't worry, they had reassured her. There was wiggle room built into the schedule. They would still be home on time.

With one last look at Abu Dhabi, Effie turned off her bedside lamp and settled back into her pillows. She had just closed her eyes when she was startled by a goose's honk, the alert on her phone that meant a text from her dad. Effie fumbled in the dark and read: *Wi-Fi out. All improving. Hope talk tomorrow. Lots love.*

The big window in Effie's room faced east, so the sun awakened her early. She felt better than she had when she'd gone to sleep. Overnight, a plan had formed in her brain. She would ride her bike to Penn Creek and have breakfast at the diner.

When Effie's parents had told her about spending the summer with her aunt and uncle, she had imagined doing farm chores. She would dress in overalls—same as Moriah Yoder did—spear hay bales with pitchforks, gather eggs and drive a tractor, pull weeds.

But when she'd gotten there, her aunt and uncle had had other ideas.

"I don't mind helping you," Effie had told them after the grand tour.

"Oh, no, no, no, sprite," Uncle Ted had said. "We didn't invite you here to be a hired hand."

"We have plenty of help already," Aunt Clare had said. "Two boys from down the road do the heavy stuff, and we bring in extra help for planting and harvest time."

"Your job is to have fun and get some R & R after a tough year at school," Uncle Ted added.

"Think of all the lovely peace and quiet compared to where you live in Brooklyn!" said Aunt Clare.

Effie suspected that secretly her aunt and uncle didn't want her help. After all, she didn't know how to do anything useful. And it looked as though they didn't have the patience to teach her. She was very glad she had asked her mother for a bicycle.

Getting dressed, she thought of Jasmine. Going out to breakfast was something the two of them did on weekend mornings in the city. One of their moms would come too, or Jasmine's nanny. Effie wasn't allowed to do much on her own. But here in Penn Creek things were going to be different. Since her aunt and uncle didn't know much about kids, Effie had the feeling she'd be on her own a lot.

And in that case, she had better get used to it.

From Jasmine, Effie's thoughts drifted to Moriah. *We probably couldn't have been friends anyway. We probably are much too different. What would we have talked about? Goats?*

Downstairs, the clock on the stove said 7:02. Effie knew her aunt and uncle would be outdoors watering before it got too hot. She found them with the strawberries and told them she was going into town.

"Good idea, sprite," said her uncle.

"Wear sunscreen," said her aunt.

Alfred must have heard her walk past on her way to get her bike because he looked up and bleated and gave her a nasty look. "Good morning to you, too," she said.

Then Boris hobbled toward her from the far side of the barn. He was preceded by the cloud of stink that was his special friend.

"Gross," Effie said, but she petted him and scratched his ears anyway. It wasn't his fault he smelled the way he did.

Effie got the bike out of the garage, tightened the straps of her helmet, tugged at her backpack, and thought of her parents. Earlier that day, if all had gone well, they would've been preparing to embark on an adventure too. Had it gone okay? Was her dad flying over the Arabian Sea right this very minute? Solar planes fly much slower than jet-powered ones. The first leg of the trip would take about twenty hours.

She knew—without wanting to think about it— that if things went terribly wrong, her aunt and uncle would find out and phone her. If all went well, she would talk to her parents later.

Same as the day before, Effie turned the bike left at the bottom of the driveway. Today, though, she was going about three miles beyond the Yoders', and soon she had sailed past their mailbox. After that came a couple of dilapidated houses, a small dairy farm that smelled like Boris, an abandoned church with peeling paint, a blue house so new it seemed to have fallen from the sky, and a barn-red house, old and sagging, with a sign out front that said FIREWOOD.

Effie had been to Penn Creek with her aunt and uncle, of course, but never by herself till now. The town's northern boundary was the creek itself, spanned by a one-lane bridge. With no cars in sight, Effie rolled across slowly so she could take in the view of mossy boulders and dull green water below.

On the town side of the bridge was a mini-mart with a neglected sign out front, its missing letters like missing teeth: AIT & T KLE & OL SOD . OME ON IN!

Beyond that was a flat-roofed church made of stucco. In its parking lot was a similar sign, but this one had all its letters: GOD HELP ME BE THE PERSON MY DOG THINKS I AM.

Effie was glad she had paused to pet Boris.

Past those buildings, the highway became Main Street, with storefronts on either side, some boarded up. On the square in the center of town, the courthouse and city hall shared a building. Made of brick with a squat white bell tower, it had two stories but looked taller because of the steps leading to the entrance doors. Effie counted five people on the sidewalks that morning.

Where is everybody? she wondered, thinking of the crowded sidewalks at home.

Effie had entered Penn Creek from the north. The diner was located at the other end of town. The sign that ran the length of its roof read THE ALPHA AND OMEGA OF PENN CREEK.

What does that mean? Effie wondered as she turned into the parking lot and rolled to a stop. Only after her feet were on the asphalt did she notice that the restaurant was dark inside, and no cars were around. A hand-lettered sign taped to the glass door explained: CLOSED FOR SUMMER VACATION. SEE YOU JULY 5.

Now what? Effie thought, doubly annoyed because her stomach was growling. *Stupid small town!* She pictured a breakfast of peanut butter crackers and chocolate milk from the mini-mart. And what was she supposed to do after that?

She could check on her parents' trip. She could read. She could play games on her tablet, post photos of Alfred the Goat to Instagram, call Jasmine.

Was the whole summer going to be like this?

Effie felt desperate. She needed something to do.

Operating on reflex, she pulled out her phone, opened Yelp, and found something surprising: *Sadie's Books, 240 W. Locust St. Books, coffee, stationery. OPEN NOW.*

The one review—from somebody named Maureen—was five stars and wordy. *It'll be faster to go there than to read all this,* she thought.

And she was right.

Penn Creek was so small you could ride a bike from end to end in five minutes—even if you weren't that good on a bike yet. Three minutes after she put her phone away, Effie rode into the parking lot of Sadie's Books.

On a street of vacant lots and run-down mobile homes, the freshly painted store looked almost magical. On either side of glass entrance doors were big, clean picture windows with colorful displays of bestsellers. Over the door was a professionally made sign that read SADIE'S in red cursive and BOOKS in black block letters.

The only vehicle in the parking lot was a blue van, so Effie was glad to see lights on inside, glad when the door yielded to her push, glad to hear the bell that tinkled as she crossed the threshold. All of a sudden she had a good feeling. Finding Sadie's might be like finding a friend.

11

Inside, the store was bright and busy with books and other interesting things. Old Motown music played from unseen speakers. In an easy chair by the front door sat a black-and-white cat, which raised its pink nose as Effie approached.

"Hello, cat." Effie tickled it between the ears. "Are you in charge here?"

The cat didn't answer, just washed its face. Effie could smell coffee. *If there's coffee, I bet there're cookies or something else a hungry person could eat for breakfast,* she thought. "Hello?" she called.

"Hello?" someone answered. It was a man, and he sounded surprised.

"Where are you?" Effie asked.

"Here," said the man at the same time his head popped up from behind a counter.

Effie held out her hand. "I'm Effie Starr Zook," she said. "It's very nice to meet you. Do you have any cookies? I have been riding my bike."

"Pendleton Odbody," said the man.

"Huh," said Effie. Was this the man's name? Or was he speaking another language, a language in which "Pendleton Odbody" meant "Yes, we have cookies," or "Sadly, no cookies today."

"I'm confused," Effie said. "Is your name Pendleton Odbody?"

"It is now," the man answered. He was broad-shouldered with a mass of black braids that tumbled to his shoulders. He was dressed in khakis and a long-sleeved button-down shirt made from the puckery fabric called seersucker. He wore square glasses with wire frames. He was black.

Effie herself was white. So were her aunt and uncle. So was Moriah's family. So, now that she thought about it, was every other person she had seen since she'd arrived in Central Pennsylvania. This was something she had not thought about till now. Besides the abundance of green and the lack of crowds, it was another difference between here and where she lived in Brooklyn.

What's up with that? she wondered.

But it probably wasn't something to mention to Mr. Odbody at this exact moment. After all, they hardly knew each other. So what she said was, "Oatmeal cookies would be good. My uncle Ted says they are healthier than other kinds because they have fiber, and fiber aids the digestion. My uncle calls me 'sprite.' I don't know why. I haven't eaten breakfast."

Mr. Odbody's response was to raise his eyebrows, and Effie was afraid he might think she was the kind of person who only went to bookstores to eat. "I also like to read," she added.

"Well, that's a good thing," said Mr. Odbody, "because I happen to carry books. And I have oatmeal cookies, too. Would you like a cup of coffee?"

Effie thought coffee was gross, but Mr. Odbody dressed so nicely that she wanted to impress him with her maturity.

"That would be lovely," she said. "And I brought

money, just in case you were worrying that I might be penniless."

"I wasn't worrying," he said. "Besides, I don't mind extending credit to good customers."

"How do you know I'm a good customer?" Effie asked. Then she remembered what Mr. Yoder had said about this being a small town and her mom and aunt being celebrities. "Oh—do you know my family?"

"Your aunt and uncle own this building," he said, and when Effie looked surprised, he added, "They own quite a few properties in town. But I can't really say I know them. I just send the rent check every month. Anyway, that's not why I think you're a good customer. I'm trusting my gut on that one." He smiled.

Effie smiled back.

Mr. Odbody put two cookies on a plate and poured a mug of coffee. "Have a seat in our two-table café. Do you mind if I join you?"

"Not at all," Effie said, doing her best to talk the way her mother and aunt did. When he sat down, she asked, "Is it pleasant to work in a bookstore?"

"It would be more pleasant if I didn't have bills to pay," Mr. Odbody said.

Effie's rosy vision of herself as benevolent fairy princess returned. "I can buy some books besides the coffee and cookies," she said.

Mr. Odbody laughed. "The coffee and cookies are on the house. But I do keep my young readers section stocked. One of my best customers is about your age. She likes high drama—*The Hunger Games*, that kind of thing."

"I'm reading *Pippi Longstocking*," Effie said. "It has drama. There's a pirate. Have you read any good books lately?"

"*Anna Karenina*," said Mr. Odbody, "for about the tenth time. It's about unhappy families."

Effie remembered seeing *Anna Karenina* around her house when her mother's book club was reading it. "That book is really long," she recalled, "and it's sad. Are you sad?"

"Not right this minute," said Mr. Odbody.

Effie decided coffee tasted okay with sugar in it, and the cookies were delicious. While she ate, she asked Mr. Odbody polite questions about himself. He was thirty-five. He had been married once. Not anymore. No kids. Originally from Johnstown,

Pennsylvania, which was in Cambria County, about seventy miles away. His grandmother—Sadie Pendleton—had lived on a farm near Penn Creek. He had named the bookstore after her because she loved to read. His favorite movie was *It's a Wonderful Life*.

"My goodness," he said at last. "I'm not usually such a talker. And now I've got books to unpack. You feel free to take your time, though, and look around. Let me know what you find."

Sadie's Books had an excellent selection of children's classics. Effie pulled *The Tale of Peter Rabbit* from the shelf and reread it. Then she looked at her favorite poems from *Now We Are Six* by A.A. Milne. Next to a book she had read and liked, *Saffy's Angel*, she found a series called The Exiles, written by the same author. Effie had a credit card with her name on it, and she always carried cash for what her parents called "incidentals." She didn't know if books counted as incidentals or not, but she paid cash for the paperbacks.

Mr. Odbody rang up the purchase. "What will you do with the rest of your day? Penn Creek must be dull compared to New York City," he said.

"I'm not sure," Effie said. "I have to check in with

my parents. I guess you know about their trip. And maybe I'll finish *Pippi Longstocking*."

"Sometime you might want to go to the Museum of the Town of Penn Creek," said Mr. Odbody. "It's hardly the Met, but there is a room devoted to your great-grandfather. Most people say he put this town on the map."

"He was a great man," said Effie. "And Mr. Yoder told me that thing about putting the town on the map. Do you know Mr. Yoder?"

"Beards for America—BFA," said Mr. Odbody.

"That's the one," she said. "Will you vote for him for mayor?"

"Probably not," said Mr. Odbody.

"My aunt says he's worse than a rattlesnake," said Effie.

"I don't know about that," Mr. Odbody said. "You're pretty well informed for someone who's only been in town a few days."

"I ask a lot of questions," Effie said.

"I noticed that," Mr. Odbody said.

"I have one more, too," Effie said. "Is it okay if I come back tomorrow?"

CHAPTER

12

It was okay.

And it was okay for her to come back the day after that and the day after that. In fact, Effie's days settled into a happy routine. She spent her mornings at Sadie's Books and her afternoons checking *Sunspot I*'s progress, chatting with Jasmine, reading, and taking walks around Zook Farm with Boris.

Her aunt and uncle she saw mainly at hors d'oeuvres time. Because she could tell they were worried about something—something to do with deeds and titles and all those boring grown-up words—she gave up pestering them with questions.

In fact, their conversations became what her parents

would have called civilized. They talked about current events and books and movies. They talked about geography and the places her parents were visiting. Before they had settled down at Zook Farm, her aunt and uncle had traveled all over the world. If Effie named a place on the map, they had a story to tell.

As always, they were nice to her. Her uncle gave her two cherries; her aunt asked about her day. Did they listen when she answered? It was hard to tell. Anyway, they never asked for details, and somehow Effie never got around to mentioning Sadie's. At first there was no particular reason for that. Later, she liked the idea of Sadie's being something private. It wasn't really a secret. It was just something she kept to herself.

Meanwhile, Mr. Odbody showed her how to work the cash register and the coffee machine, taught her the prices of the baked goods, let her read advance copies of new kids' books and decide which ones he ought to stock. She fed the bookstore cat, whose name was Chop Suey. She let him nap in her lap while she read.

Sometimes when there were no customers, they listened to baseball games on the radio. Mr. Odbody had played in college, and Effie played softball. Mr. Odbody was a Pirates fan. Effie rooted for the Mets. They agreed to disagree.

"I feel bad that I can't pay you when you've been so much help," Mr. Odbody said one day.

"It's a whole lot better than doing nothing," Effie told him. "Besides, my family is well fixed."

Mr. Odbody laughed. "That's an expression you don't hear much. But a person, well fixed or not, should be paid for her labor."

"Can I ask you something?" Effie said.

"You always do," Mr. Odbody said.

"How come you opened a nice bookstore in such a small town? Wouldn't it do better in a city?"

"As I think I mentioned, my grandmother lived around here," Mr. Odbody replied. "So I wanted to see what the town was all about. Also, I got a good deal on the space. This building started out as an auto garage, and then it became an antique store. For a long while, it was empty. Your aunt and uncle were happy to have me come in and fix it up."

"Do you worry when there's not much business?" Effie asked him.

Mr. Odbody shrugged. "Everyone worries," he said, "but I have reason to believe that brighter times are just around the corner."

Some days Sadie's had more customers than others. Tourists stopped by, most of them city people who thought Penn Creek was picturesque. A frequent customer was Mrs. Patrick McMinty, the widow of the mayor who had died shoveling snow and also the "Maureen" who had written the review on Yelp.

Mrs. McMinty did not match Effie's expectations about widows. She wasn't weepy; she was talkative. She carried herself grandly, even though her lipstick was often applied unevenly, and her usual outfit was sneakers with baggy shorts and T-shirts bearing messages like VOTE GOP. If she was sad living alone, she kept it to herself.

Effie thought Mrs. McMinty must be about Grandpa Bob's age—the age he would've been, that is, if he weren't dead. Aunt Clare and Mom had been the only children of his first marriage, which broke up when they were little. As adults, they saw him only rarely. When he died, he was wed to Wife No. 5, and

Wives No. 2–4 had given him additional children. He used to laugh when he said he could hardly keep track.

Grandpa Bob had put in an appearance at Effie's christening—there was a photo to prove it. But with so many other grandchildren and step-grandchildren, he had never seen Effie again. Some years he, or the current wife, had remembered to send a birthday card.

Now Effie wondered if Grandpa Bob could have something to do with the bad blood. She knew for sure that he was born in Los Angeles and moved with his parents to Zook Farm when he was little. Putting all this together, Effie asked Mrs. McMinty if she had known him or his parents—her great-grandparents in other words, Gus and Effie Zook.

"Yes, indeed." Mrs. McMinty was sitting at a chair in the bookstore's two-table café. Effie had just refilled her mug of coffee. "Your grandfather, may he rest in peace, went to high school here with me. Of course he was several years ahead of me. He couldn't wait to get away, to move back to California, and that is just what he did."

"California is where my mom and my aunt are from," Effie said.

Mrs. McMinty nodded. "But I used to see them sometimes when they came to visit their grandparents. My goodness, those girls were adorable." She sighed. "So unfortunate about Gus and Effie's marriage in the end."

Effie's ears perked up. Was this a clue to Effie the First's sad photograph? "What happened to their marriage?"

Mrs. McMinty's face froze momentarily. Then she took a quick sip of coffee. "Nothing," she said. "Nothing at all. Forget I mentioned it."

"How am I supposed to do that?" Effie asked.

"Try holding your breath," Mrs. McMinty said. "If you deprive your brain of oxygen, it will cause your memory to fail."

"I never heard that before," Effie said.

"No, you wouldn't have," Mrs. McMinty said, "because I just made it up. Still, it stands to reason it might work."

Effie agreed but didn't test the theory. She didn't actually want to forget what Mrs. McMinty had said.

There is a secret in Penn Creek, she thought, *and there is a conspiracy of grown-ups to hide it too. What is it they don't want me to know?*

Washing the dishes that day, she considered the clues. Her great-grandmother's sadness was one. The bad blood between her family and the Yoders was another—especially added to Mr. Yoder's admiration for Gus Zook. Now there was also Mrs. McMinty's comment about something unfortunate in her great-grandparents' marriage.

What did it all add up to, anyway?

Effie dried the dishes, then put the plates back on the shelf and the mugs back on their hooks. Wiping down the counter, she thought of something else. It was mysterious too, but probably unrelated.

Why hadn't her aunt and uncle ever told her about Sadie's Books or brought her here? Was it only another case of their not knowing what a kid might like?

Or was it part of the secret?

13

The week before the Fourth of July, Mrs. McMinty came into Sadie's carrying a flyer for the Penn Creek Annual Fourthfest.

Effie was behind the counter at the two-table café. "I can tack that up on our bulletin board," she offered.

Mrs. McMinty thanked her. "Are you planning to go?"

"If my aunt and uncle will take me," Effie said.

"It is not to be missed," said Mrs. McMinty.

"Would you like a cup of tea?" Mr. Odbody came in from the storeroom with a carton of books, which he set down on his desk. "The tea is on the house today."

"Don't mind if I do." Mrs. McMinty made herself comfortable at a table. "But if you give your wares away, how will this place ever stay in business?"

"The important thing is to keep good customers coming back," said Mr. Odbody. "Effie, do you mind getting the tea?"

"Sure thing," said Effie.

"There's a question I've been meaning to ask." Mrs. McMinty turned her chair to face Mr. Odbody. "Long ago, there was a woman by the name of Pendleton who lived in Penn Creek."

"Was there?" Mr. Odbody was busy opening the carton of books.

Effie brought over a tray with hot water and tea bags. "Thank you, dear," Mrs. McMinty said, "and yes, indeed there was. Here is the interesting thing. Like you, this woman was of the African American persuasion."

From Mr. Odbody's throat came a sound like a stifled belch, which soon became a coughing fit.

"Are you okay?" Effie asked. "Can I get you a glass of water?"

Still coughing, Mr. Odbody nodded. Effie got

him the water. While he drank, Effie turned to Mrs. McMinty and said, "I don't think 'African American persuasion' is the right way to say that."

"I was trying to be culturally sensitive," Mrs. McMinty said.

Mr. Odbody cleared his throat. "I believe we all share the same culture," he said. "As for my skin, 'black' will do, even though 'chocolate brown' would be more accurate."

"I think you are a very nice color, Mr. Odbody," said Effie.

"I think you are a nice color too," said Mr. Odbody.

"My great-grandmother was Greek," said Effie. "It was a long time ago, but I take after her."

"Heredity's a funny thing," said Mr. Odbody. "There's no telling which ancestor a person might favor."

Now Mrs. McMinty cleared her throat. Effie had already noticed she did not like to be left out of conversations. "As I was saying," she went on. "There was this family here called Pendleton. Do you suppose you could be related?"

Mr. Odbody shrugged. "Pennsylvania is a big

state, with a good-sized black population, even if not so many live right around here."

Mrs. McMinty nodded. "That's true. I just wondered because of the names being the same."

"Mr. Odbody," said Effie, "wouldn't that woman be your—"

"Effie!" Mr. Odbody interrupted so sharply that Effie was startled.

"What?" she said.

"Uh . . . be careful with that boiling water, now," he said. "I, uh . . . wouldn't want you to burn yourself."

Effie frowned. "I'm not anywhere near—," she started to say, but then she saw the look on Mr. Odbody's face and changed course. "Right. Sorry. I'll be extra careful."

What was that all about? Effie asked herself. *Mr. Odbody doesn't want Mrs. McMinty to know about his grandmother, I guess. But why not? Is this a clue to something too?*

After that Effie could hardly wait for Mrs. McMinty to leave so she could ask what was going on.

Nearby, at the same time, something else was happening.

A couple of miles north of the Penn Creek town limits, a woman wearing pale blue sweats called, "Leaving now!" and retrieved her car keys from the hook by the door.

"Wait a sec!" Her daughter, dressed in overalls and a ball cap as usual, came running down the stairs. "Can't you take me with you?" she said. "Please, Mama? E.J.'s out on the tractor with Luke. I can visit Sadie's while Ava does your hair."

Anjelica Yoder took a breath and let it out slowly. Her husband would have kittens if he knew she sometimes took Moriah to the bookstore. But she herself had loved to read as a girl, and there was no library in town. Besides, there was nothing for her husband to worry about. Moriah was much too sensible to be disturbed by crazy ideas from books.

"Oh, all right, but not a word to your papa."

"I *know*, Mama," the girl said. "What do you think—I've gone off my rocker?"

14

I n the history of the universe, no one ever drank a mug of tea as slowly as Mrs. McMinty did that day.

At least, that was how it seemed to Effie.

It was noon by the time the bookstore's best customer had finished the last dregs and departed, finally freeing Effie to ask Mr. Odbody what was going on. "Why don't you want Mrs. McMinty to know about your grandmother?" she said.

"What about my grandmother?" Mr. Odbody said.

"I don't know *what* about your grandmother. That's my whole point!" Effie said. "That she lived here? That her name was Sadie Pendleton? That she was of the 'African American persuasion'?"

Mr. Odbody grinned. "She wasn't one hundred percent of that particular persuasion. She was what today we'd call biracial. Then they would've said mulatto—half white and half black."

"Yeah, okay, whatever," said Effie. "But what I want to know is if she was some kind of secret."

Mr. Odbody shrugged. "I don't like everyone in town discussing my business, and Mrs. McMinty, you will have noticed, is a talker."

This was true, but Effie had the feeling he was leaving something out. Was Mr. Odbody part of the great grown-up conspiracy too?

Effie tried to think up a new and better question, but before she could the entrance bell tinkled, and in walked Moriah Yoder.

"Hello, Chop Suey." Moriah paused to pet the cat, who was curled up in an easy chair near the front of the store. Then she looked around. "Mr. O?" she called.

"Present and accounted for." Mr. Odbody waved.

Moriah turned toward him and saw Effie. Moriah's eyes widened. For a split second the girls' happy expressions were identical, a fact that seemed to cement some wordless bargain. Bad blood between their families or not, Effie Zook and Moriah Yoder were going to be friends.

Pendleton Odbody looked from one girl to the other and shook his head. "The two of you together?" he said. "That's gotta be trouble."

Suddenly Effie realized something. "Moriah's the girl you told me about who likes bloody books, isn't she? I met her one time before. She lives on the other side of the woods from my aunt and uncle."

"I know where she lives," Mr. Odbody said. "Moriah, there's a new one in the Grisly Ghost series coming out soon. I should have it next time you come in. Would you like something to eat?"

"I can get it for her, Mr. Odbody," Effie said. "Would you care for a cup of coffee, miss?"

"On the house," said Mr. Odbody.

"I can pay." Moriah walked back to the café and sat down. "This time of year, Dad pays E.J. and me for washing lettuce. Luke and Adam sell it at the farmers' market in Millheim. Later in the summer we box up berries and shuck corn. There's a lot to do, so I have spending money."

"Luke and Adam are your other brothers." Effie put cookies on a plate. "How old are they again?"

"High school," Moriah said. "In the summer, they work all the time."

"So your family farms too, same as Aunt Clare and Uncle Ted," said Effie.

"It's only a side business," said Moriah. "My pa has a regular job in IT—you know, computers."

Effie assumed Moriah must be making a joke. People with computer jobs lived in cities and had a lot of education. They didn't wear overalls and believe beards make you strong.

Did they?

"What kind of computer job?" Effie asked.

"Inventory control," Moriah said.

"Oh!" Effie said, and immediately changed her mind. No kid could make that up. "But I thought he was running for mayor. If he's elected, will he quit?"

"He talks about quitting sometimes," Moriah said. "He thinks soon he might be able to. But you don't get paid to be mayor of Penn Creek. You just go to meetings and give speeches."

Effie shook her head. "I don't understand grown-ups. Who would want to do that?"

Mr. Odbody had returned to his desk on the other side of the store by this time. Even so, he overheard the conversation. "I can answer that question," he said. "Power."

Effie brought the tray of cookies and coffee to Moriah. "That's preposterous," she told him. "How does going to meetings and giving speeches in Penn Creek get you power?"

"It is not preposterous!" said Mr. Odbody, and Effie hoped she hadn't hurt his feelings.

"My pa is a big thinker," Moriah said. "He hopes that once he has the title of mayor, more people will pay attention. Plus, Penn Creek might give him a place to put some of the precepts into practice."

Effie frowned. "Does he want to wash feet?"

"Hygiene is very important, Effie," said Moriah. "My pa wants to outlaw shoes indoors and install foot-washing stations too."

"As a business owner, I'm not so sure about that last part," said Mr. Odbody. "What if people are so busy washing their feet that they don't have time to shop?"

"What are his other ideas?" Effie asked. "Like, what's the deal with beards?"

"Precept One," Moriah recited. "A man's beard is a signifier of his special place in the natural order of things."

"What about the special place of women?" Effie wanted to know.

"That's Precept Two," said Moriah. "A woman has her own special place in the natural order of things."

Effie didn't like the sound of that. Did it mean women were supposed to stay stuck in their places? But maybe that was unfair. She asked some more questions. What exactly did "precept" mean, anyway? (It was a cross between a belief and a rule.) How many precepts were there? (Two hundred and three, as of breakfast.) Where did the precepts come from?

When Moriah said some of them had come from a wise man who'd lived long ago, Effie remembered something. "That was my great-great-grandfather, Gus Zook!" she said. "He was a great man. Your dad read some stuff he wrote and borrowed his ideas."

Moriah shook her head. "Now *you're* being preposterous."

"I'm not," said Effie, and she repeated what her aunt and uncle had told her.

Moriah was frowning. "That doesn't make sense. My family and your family—"

"Bad blood," Effie said. "Something happened a long time ago."

"I know," Moriah said, "but I don't know what."

"Do you know, Mr. Odbody?" Effie turned in her chair to look at him.

Mr. Odbody rested his elbows on his desk and leaned forward. "Let me get this straight," he said. "Moriah's dad read something Mr. Zook wrote, and from it got his big ideas. Am I right?"

"I think so," said Effie.

"Well, I'll be darned. Reading is dangerous!" Mr. Odbody said, but he added—before Moriah could object—"I'm kidding. I mean, I may not be a fan of mandatory foot washing. But don't I own a book-store? I *am* a fan of reading. And come to think of it, I have some precepts of my own."

"Like what?" Effie asked.

"Like ice cream is good for you," said Mr. Odbody, "and, uh . . . it's more important to think deep thoughts than it is to have a lot of money."

"I like those precepts," said Effie. "I guess I have one too. If you don't pick up pennies, you will have bad luck."

Moriah pursed her lips. "Those are not real precepts like my papa's," she said.

"There's room in this world for lots of kinds of precepts," Mr. Odbody said.

Effie thought this seemed obvious, but Moriah shook her head. "That's not what Papa says. He says only a few ideas are good, and everybody should agree on them and pull together."

"Is that a precept too?" Mr. Odbody asked.

"Number one forty-three," said Moriah.

Now that she had talked to Moriah for a while, Effie thought maybe she understood her new friend's peculiar behavior the day they first met.

"Are the precepts the reason you're not supposed to talk to strangers?" Effie asked. "Is it because strangers might have different precepts—different ideas, I mean?"

Moriah nodded. "Outside ideas are dangerous, especially for kids because kids' minds are weak."

"My mind is not weak!" Effie said.

"Don't take offense, Effie," Moriah said. "It isn't your fault. It takes years to understand the precepts and live them without questioning. Till you're old enough, it's dangerous to 'engage too much with the outside world.' That's how Papa says it."

"But how can you stand not to ask questions?" Effie said. "I always have a lot of questions."

Moriah sighed. "Me too. Papa says that's how he knows I'm not grown up yet."

Mr. Odbody pushed his chair back from the desk. "No offense, but that's a bunch of malarkey," he said.

Moriah narrowed her eyes. "It is not," she said.

"Well, I can't very well take it back, can I?" Mr. Odbody said. "I own a bookstore. Almost every single thing I sell is full of ideas. I'd be out of business if people didn't want them."

"But according to Papa, most ideas are bad ideas," Moriah said.

"Good ideas, bad ideas—you can't keep any of 'em down," said Mr. Odbody. "So what you do is let them duke it out. The good ones will win in a fair fight. I guess that's one of my precepts too."

Moriah frowned. "That's not what Papa says."

"I don't suppose so," said Mr. Odbody.

"Agree to disagree?" said Effie.

Moriah didn't look happy, but she said, "I guess."

Effie said, "Good, because I have one more question. Did you get in trouble the day I came over?"

"I had to recite fifty precepts before dinner," Moriah said. "I'm good at memorizing. It could've been worse. But I have questions for you, too. Can I ask 'em? Fair is fair."

Moriah wanted to know about Brooklyn, Effie's house, Effie's friends, Effie's school. Effie thought Mr. Yoder would have found their conversation to be very dangerous, but she didn't say that to Moriah.

When it was time for Moriah to leave to meet her mom, Effie asked how the two of them were going to stay in touch. She knew Moriah didn't have a phone. She didn't want to lose her.

Moriah didn't have a good answer. "All we can do is hope we run into each other same as today."

"But what if it's an emergency?" Effie asked.

Moriah thought for a moment. "You could tie a scarf on a branch of the hemlock tree. It's the tallest one in the woods between our houses. Hang it high as you can, and I will see it."

"What color scarf?" Effie asked.

"Pink," said Moriah.

"What if I can't find a pink scarf?"

"Effie," Moriah said patiently, "if I see any color scarf in the tree, I'll figure there's an emergency, and I will come."

15

Effie did not tell her aunt and uncle she had seen Moriah. And she didn't tell her parents that night when they talked on Skype.

By now there were five pushpins on Effie's map, each one marking a stopover on *Sunspot I*'s route. That day her mom and dad were in China. After a rest day, it would be her dad's turn to fly across the East China Sea to Japan.

"Are you having fun?" Effie asked the two of them. They were scrunched together so Effie could see them both at the same time on her tablet.

"Sure, we are," said her mom.

"We aren't in this for fun," said her dad.

"I know, Dad," said Effie. "You've told me a hundred times. You are pioneers, like the Wright brothers. Someday because of you everyone will fly in solar airplanes."

"Exactly right," said her mom. "So tell us, how's Zook Farm? Are you going to Fourthfest?"

"How do you know about Fourthfest?" Effie said.

"When we were kids, Clare and I used to go to Penn Creek in the summer. You know that," her mom said.

"Yeah, but I didn't know that Fourthfest was that old," Effie said.

"Ouch," said her mom.

"I don't mean you're old," Effie said. "I mean—"

"Only teasing," said her mom. "Your great-grandfather started Fourthfest. Did you know that?"

"For reals?" Effie said.

"For reals," said her mom. "He was a great man."

"I know," said Effie.

"I hate to break this up," said her dad, "but rest day or not, we've got a lot to do. We've had some trouble with the batteries, and I want to do some testing before we move on."

Effie did not like the sound of that. "What trouble with the batteries?"

"Nothing for you to worry about," her mom said. "It will all work out fine. *Sunspot I* is doing great, and we are having fun."

"See you soon, Ef," her dad said.

"See you soon, Dad. Bye, Mom. Love you!"

Effie turned out her light a few minutes later. The only sounds were crickets chirping and the occasional hum of a car on the road. Her bed was soft, and the day at last had released its heat. She was perfectly comfortable. But she couldn't fall asleep.

She was thinking. Didn't her family have precepts too? Just like Moriah's?

Gus Zook was a great man.

Everything works out fine.

Her parents were aviation pioneers like the Wright brothers.

Still, there is a difference between my family and Moriah's, Effie thought. *My family isn't crazy.*

Is it?

• • •

When Effie told Aunt Clare and Uncle Ted that she wanted to go to Fourthfest, they told her not to expect too much.

"But the flyer says kettle corn, funnel cake, cheese on a stick, and cornhole," Effie informed them. "I don't even know what those things are. It will be good for me. It will be a cultural experience."

Uncle Ted explained that cornhole was a bean-bag game, and the others were salty, highly fattening foods.

"If we're going, we should leave at seven, so we have plenty of time to eat ourselves into an early grave before the fireworks start," he added.

"Oh dear," said Aunt Clare.

The evening was typically warm and muggy for July. The squirrels snagged bedtime snacks as cicadas tuned up in the trees. Everyone looked forward to the fireflies. Effie had never seen the town of Penn Creek so crowded. Every parking spot was taken for blocks. It was a long, long walk from the truck to the square. There, in the shadow of the courthouse tower, white canopies had popped up like mushrooms. Jewelry and other crafts were on sale, as well as baked goods, silk flowers, and photographs of Amish barns. You could buy equipment for brewing your own beer, look at brochures for a new subdivision on old farmland, or sit fully clothed in a dry, empty Jacuzzi.

"Oh, look—pony rides!" Aunt Clare pointed at a man leading a spotted pony in a circle, a grinning toddler on its back. "Your mother and I used to love those, Effie. Do you want one?"

"I am too big for a pony ride, Aunt Clare," said Effie.

"What if I want a pony ride?" asked Uncle Ted.

"You are also too big," said Aunt Clare.

"In that case, may I have an ice-cream cone?" Uncle Ted asked.

Distracted by a display of earrings in vegetable shapes, Aunt Clare didn't answer.

"I'll buy you an ice-cream cone," said Effie.

"Thank you," said Uncle Ted, who chose butter pecan. Effie had a single scoop of strawberry. They walked past a picnic pavilion, more jewelry sellers, and an endless selection of coffee mugs. Finally, Effie saw a banner that read BEARDS FOR AMERICA on a white canopy decked out with bunting, pinwheels, twinkle lights, and flags. In front were signs for various precepts:

NO. 67: IT TAKES BOTH KING AND QUEEN TO MAKE A HAPPY CASTLE.

NO. 202: KEEP YOUR EYE ON THE BALL OR IT WILL SMACK YOU IN THE HEAD.

NO. 151: THE FUTURE CARES AS MUCH ABOUT YOUR WRONGS AS YOUR RIGHTS.

NO. 58: HE WHO HOLDS THE WHIP DRIVES THE BUGGY.

Effie looked around for Moriah but didn't see her. In fact, she saw no one of what Mrs. McMinty would call the female persuasion. Instead, she saw a cluster of men around Mr. Yoder. Most of them had beards, though none was as splendid as his own.

"Don't stare, Effie." Aunt Clare took her arm. "Wouldn't you like a deep-fried Snickers bar? Your mother wouldn't like it if I only gave you ice cream for dinner."

Effie did want a deep-fried Snickers bar! And deep-fried pickles and deep-fried cheese on a stick too! But before she turned away from the BFA canopy,

a small person flew out from under it and sprinted—
bang—right into Effie's knees.

"Effie Starr Zook!" hollered the person, who
turned out to be E.J. Yoder. "Do you remember me?"

"Of course," Effie said, giving E.J. a hug at the
same time she looked around for his dad. She didn't
want E.J. to get in trouble. Unfortunately, Mr. Yoder
had seen his son bolt and already was striding toward
them.

"Come on back to the tent, E.J." Mr. Yoder's smile
was tense. "Let's leave these people to enjoy their holiday."

"I'm talking, Papa," said E.J. "Zooks aren't all
bad. Effie gave me berry juice that time."

Mr. Yoder put his hand on his son's shoulder.
"Very generous of her. Come on back to the tent
now."

"You come along too, Effie," said Uncle Ted. "We
wouldn't want you to starve. What did you say about
a Snickers bar?"

"I want a Snickers bar!" said E.J. "Can't I have
one, Pa?"

"No," his father told him. "Now, I am going to

count to ten, young man, and you will move your—"

"No, I won't," said E.J. "I want Snickers." And before anyone could stop him, he had ducked out from under his father's hand and run for it.

Had Mr. Yoder chased his son, he would have caught up right away. Instead he followed his first instinct, which was to holler, "You come back here, E.J.!"

E.J. did not.

Soon he was halfway across the lawn, and moments after that he had disappeared into the crowd.

"Oh dear," said Aunt Clare.

"I'll get him," said Effie, and she jogged across the lawn herself. She had gotten lost once when she was E.J.'s age. It was in a store at Christmas. It was scary. She hated to think of E.J. scared now, dodging blindly among all the tall people.

Effie ran up the courthouse steps and stood looking out over the crowd. So many people. So many little kids. The light in the sky was fading.

"E.J.? Where are you?" she called.

"Here I am, Effie." He tugged on her T-shirt from behind.

"Oh, thank goodness. Don't do that anymore! Your dad won't spank you, will he?"

E.J. shrugged. "I dunno. If he does, I can take it."

"It's not right to spank kids," Effie said.

"Do your parents spank you?" E.J. asked.

"Of course not," said Effie.

"So how do you know?" E.J. asked.

Effie opened her mouth and closed it again. She didn't have an answer. Then Mr. Yoder appeared with Aunt Clare and Uncle Ted right behind.

"You worried me half to death!" Mr. Yoder told E.J. "There are bad people in the world—you know that! Now, don't you *ever, ever, ever, ever—*"

"Ever," supplied E.J. "And I only wanted a Snickers bar."

Without further ado, Mr. Yoder grabbed a handful of E.J.'s T-shirt and lifted him off the ground. "You are coming back to the BFA tent with me, and there you will sit, silent and still, until it is time to go home."

At first E.J. flailed, swimming in the air, but after a few steps he gave up and floated along for the ride.

Effie felt bad—no deep-fried Snickers bar for that

kid—but a few seconds later he spun around to look at her. One thumb was in his mouth; with his other hand he waved.

Effie remembered how E.J. had tugged Alfred the Goat's black beard. *That,* she thought, *is either a bad little kid or a brave one.*

16

Effie enjoyed her Snickers bar and then, for the sake of good health, a basket of battered, deep-fried cauliflower with ranch dressing on the side. While she was eating, her aunt and uncle greeted a handful of friends, then introduced their niece. Through mouthfuls of hot, half-chewed cauliflower, she tried to say "nice to meet you."

Once or twice, she thought she noticed people looking at the three of them and pointing. Hadn't Mr. Yoder called her mom and aunt celebrities? With her parents' big trip in the news, she supposed she was one too—even though neither Mr. Odbody nor Mrs. McMinty treated her that way.

And speaking of Mrs. McMinty, Effie and Aunt Clare and Uncle Ted had just sat down and arranged themselves on a blanket to watch the fireworks when she came striding toward them. She was wearing her trademark baggy shorts and sneakers with a T-shirt that read YANKEE DOODLE GIRL. In honor of the holiday, her lipstick was redder than usual.

"No need to get up!" she called.

Aunt Clare murmured, "Oh dear," and scrambled to her feet. "I don't think we've seen you since the memorial service. How have you been, Maureen?"

"The mayor was a wonderful man," said Uncle Ted, also on his feet.

"As well as can be expected after fifty years of marriage," said Mrs. McMinty. "The trick is to keep busy. That's something you two know about. There's nothing more absorbing than real estate, is there? I'm sure it's a lovely distraction having your niece to brighten your days. I've enjoyed getting to know her."

Mrs. McMinty smiled at Effie, who by this time was also standing. She didn't know what Mrs. McMinty was talking about, but she did know one thing. Her visits to Sadie's would not be private much longer. "It is very nice knowing you too," she said.

Uncle Ted looked quizzically at Effie, who shrugged and mouthed, *Tell you later.*

Mrs. McMinty continued talking to Aunt Clare. "What all Penn Creek wants to know," she said, "is how much are you planning to sell? Prices are tumbling, and that's bad for all us property owners."

"I know it," said Aunt Clare, "and we're keeping that in mind. We wouldn't be selling at all if we didn't have to."

"I suppose not," said Mrs. McMinty. "And I suppose you won't choose this moment to tell me what's going on either. It's all the girls in the bridge club talk about."

"No," said Aunt Clare. "This is not the right moment."

"Didn't think so," said Mrs. McMinty. "I suppose it will come out eventually. Meanwhile, remember you do have friends in this town, and I am one of them."

"Thank you," said Aunt Clare.

Darkness was falling fast by this time; the first fireflies had appeared. There were countless stars in the country sky, but now—in the bushes and trees surrounding the lawn—the blinking fireflies seemed more numerous.

Mrs. McMinty turned to Effie. "Isn't it a lovely evening? You don't get fireflies like this in the city, do you?"

"There's hardly any," Effie said.

"Enjoy the show then, and the fireworks, too," Mrs. McMinty said. "I'm sure I'll see you soon at Sadie's."

The moment Mrs. McMinty was gone, Aunt Clare looked at her niece with wide blue eyes. Her mouth was open too. "Sadie's Books?" she said.

Effie shrugged and tried to sound casual. "I hang out there sometimes."

Uncle Ted shook his head. "And all along I thought you went to the diner. I should have realized. . . . Where did you think she was going, Clare?"

"Going?" Aunt Clare looked at Effie again. "Have you been going somewhere?"

Uncle Ted put his big hand on his niece's shoulder. "We probably should be keeping better track of you. But we're not used to children. And you're so independent."

"You don't have to be sorry," said Effie. "I am perfectly fine on my own. But what were you and Mrs. McMinty talking about? Lawyers and selling stuff?"

"Nothing important," said Aunt Clare. "Nothing at all. But, Effie, if you've been going to Sadie's . . . then I guess you've met Mr. . . . . What does he call himself, Ted?"

"Odboy," said Uncle Ted.

"Od*body*," said Effie. "And why did you say it that way? Isn't Odbody his name?"

"No," Aunt Clare said. "And you should stay away from him, Effie. He is not what he appears to be."

Effie did not believe her aunt. Mr. Odbody was her friend. He knew her better than they did, knew more about the way she thought, anyway. Without him and without Sadie's, she would never have survived this long in Penn Creek.

Effie was angry and controlled herself with an effort. "Please tell me what kind of drama."

"It's grown-up stuff," said Uncle Ted. "Boring as heck. Nothing of interest to a child."

"But I am already interested," said Effie. "Something is going on around here, and no one will tell me, and I want to know. Does it have to do with the bad blood between us and the Yoders? I know— how about if I ask my parents? Do my parents know?"

Uncle Ted was losing patience. "Effie, can you please give it a rest? Your parents are too busy for your questions right now, and frankly, so are your aunt and I. Now"—he took a breath, let it out, and tried to smile—"what do you say, sprite? Shall we sit down and enjoy ourselves?"

Effie sat, but unhappily. *I won't give it a rest,* she thought. *If I had E.J.'s courage, I would run away too. I hate grown-ups. I hate Penn Creek. I hate my parents for leaving me here.*

Effie's silent rant was interrupted by the strains of a patriotic march and a sonorous voice announcing that the fireworks were about to begin. Even the cicadas hushed momentarily before first a whistle and then a *crack* signaled the start of the show.

At home in New York City, there were so many fireworks, they blotted out the sky. Here there weren't as many, but they were a whole lot closer. Effie could follow each flare's flight from ground to treetop to bursting in air, and each one made a satisfying *boom*. It was much more spectacular than Effie had expected, spectacular enough that for a while she forgot she was mad.

CHAPTER

17

The fireflies called it a night not long after Effie fell asleep. Moonset had come early, so for a time there were only the stars to illuminate the hills and valleys. But the summer sun is never gone for long, and the land had barely caught its breath when the sky began to brighten.

Elsewhere, other things were happening.

Over the Pacific Ocean, somewhere between Japan and Hawaii, the setting sun drew magenta stripes on the horizon. It was a splendid sight, but strapped into the cockpit of *Sunspot I*, Effie's mother saw only the flashing gauges on the instrument panel. The plane was losing altitude fast. Something had gone wrong.

In Penn Creek, the driver of a blue van parked in front of a store on Locust Street and climbed out, leaving the lights on. He was a big man and strong, but moving slowly that day. He walked around to the back of the van, unlatched the doors, pulled them open, and removed a sign, its neatly painted letters still damp.

Even closer to Zook Farm, the kids of the Yoder household slept peacefully while the parents engaged in quiet discussion.

"Not much longer now," said Rob Yoder, who was combing his magnificent beard in front of the bathroom sink. "There's one last court appearance tomorrow, and then we ought to have a decision."

Standing in the bathroom doorway, Anjelica spoke to her husband's reflection in the mirror. "And after that what? It rains money?"

"I wouldn't put it that way," Rob Yoder said. "More like justice is served."

A little more than three hours later, Effie Starr Zook rode her bicycle to town as usual. The morning was hot and the sky was blue. The dew was turning to haze above the asphalt.

Falling asleep the night before, frustrated with all grown-ups everywhere but especially the ones in her own family, Effie had comforted herself by thinking of Sadie's. Maybe Mr. Odbody knew something about the legal drama. Maybe he would tell her if she asked politely. Maybe Mrs. McMinty would.

Effie rounded the corner onto Locust Street and saw immediately that something was wrong. No blue van was in the parking lot. A new white sign was in the window. Before even jumping off her bike, she read the big black letters: BOOKSTORE CLOSED. LOST OUR LEASE. APOLOGIES, PENDLETON ODBODY.

Lost our lease? Effie thought. *What does that mean exactly? Did Aunt Clare and Uncle Ted do something?*

Effie let go of her bike, and it fell with a *clunk.* The store was dark, but even so she ran up and tugged the door till it rattled. "Mr. Odbody? Open up! It's Effie!"

Inside, something stirred, but it wasn't Mr. Odbody. It wasn't even human. It was Chop Suey, who strolled into the light, looked through the glass at Effie, and meowed.

The poor thing, Effie thought. *Did Mr. Odbody forget him?*

Effie wished she had a way to get in touch with him, but she didn't know where he lived, didn't even have his phone number. She could e-mail, but he had told her once he used e-mail for store business only. Would he still be checking it?

Not knowing what else to do, Effie rode her bike around to the back of the building, where a strip of pavement was bordered by dry weeds and a sagging wooden fence. On the back wall was a sign, DELIVERIES ONLY, NO PARKING, and beside it a door that led into the storeroom. Effie leaned her bike against the building, grabbed the doorknob, and twisted.

To her great surprise, it turned.

Now what? If she walked in, would she get bopped on the head? That exact thing happened all the time to Nancy, Bess, and George.

Effie reminded herself that this was real life, straightened her shoulders, and went in. The storeroom was gloomy but only until she found the light switch, which brought to life the overhead fluorescents.

"Hello?" Effie called, and heard rustling in response. "Chop Suey? Here, kitty, kitty!"

Effie walked through a second door into the main part of the store, which was lit by daylight from the front windows. She had been here countless times, but now the space felt still and unfamiliar. It even smelled empty—book dust and the faint sad whiff of burned coffee.

Effie scanned the space, and her eyes were drawn to a white envelope on the wooden counter of the two-table café. There was writing on the envelope, Mr. Odbody's. It said: *For Effie Starr Zook.*

This is freaky, Effie thought, and a kaleidoscope of crazy ideas assailed her. The bookstore was a portal into a parallel universe where carnivorous dinosaurs were massing on Main Street. Mr. Odbody lived in a castle with a crystal ball through which he was watching her right now. In the envelope was a treasure map left by a time-traveling pirate captain.

Effie shook her head to clear it. *This,* she thought, *is what I get for reading so many books.*

She took a breath for strength, then tore open the envelope. A key fell out along with a piece of paper.

The key she picked up and put in the back pocket of her jeans. The paper she unfolded. She was hoping for something long and detailed that explained everything. What she got was this:

Dear Effie,

Please take care of Chop Suey. I will be back for him as soon as I can.

Fond regards,

Pendleton Odbody

Effie read this twice, hoping the words might seem more helpful the second time. When they didn't, she snorted and spoke to the ceiling. "Am I supposed to take Chop Suey on my handlebars or what?"

The cat must have heard his name because he sauntered up from the front of the store, stopped at Effie's feet, and washed his face. Effie knelt and scratched the spot behind his ears till he bumped his head against her palm and purred.

"I'll ask Uncle Ted to bring me back to get you," she told him. "He'll do it. He feels guilty for not keeping better track of me."

After that, Effie filled Chop Suey's water dish from the sink by the coffee counter, added cat chow to his food dish, and scooped a new layer of litter into his box.

"All done for now," she told Chop Suey. "Hang in there, and don't be lonely."

Outside, Effie pushed the heavy door shut, took the key from her pocket, tried it in the lock, and found that it fit.

Mr. Odbody knew I'd come by. He even knew I'd lock up, Effie thought. *So that's one nice thing on a terrible day. He knew he could count on me.*

There was another thought lurking around the corners of Effie's mind: Was it more than coincidence that Sadie's had closed today—one day after her aunt and uncle learned that she had been coming here?

For once Effie herself thought she had too many questions. It was time to get some answers. But she didn't know where Mr. Odbody lived, her aunt and uncle weren't helpful, and Moriah was off-limits.

Effie could think of only one place to go.

18

The Museum of the Town of Penn Creek, identified by a plaque affixed to the wrought-iron fence out front, was the best-kept old house on a tree-lined block of old houses. Out front in the driveway was a small silver car.

Effie pushed her bike up the walk and leaned it against the four steps that led to the front door. A moment later she stood in a wood-paneled entrance hall with marble tiles on the floor.

It was all really nice. No cobwebs. No dust. No damp smell.

Directly to Effie's left was a wide doorway that led into what probably used to be a sitting room. Above it was a carved wooden sign that read DEDICATED TO THE MEMORY OF GUSTAVUS AND EFFIE ZOOK. There was a staircase to the right of the doorway and beside it a desk. On the desk were a lamp, a call bell, a guest book, and a pen.

Effie signed her name in the book, noticing that she was the first visitor that day. The only other person on the page had visited the Saturday before. Effie could read only the initials of the scrawled names, T-squiggle, S-squiggle. Under hometown, he or she had written more legibly "Harrisburg."

Effie tapped the call bell and heard quick, light footsteps in response.

"Good morning! Good morning!" called a man's voice from the top of the stairs. "Why," he said when he saw her, "you're Miss Zook, aren't you?"

Effie realized she had seen the man in the crowd at the BFA booth at Fourthfest. In a sea of T-shirts, his neat polo had stood out. Also, he was one of the few men there without a beard.

"Good morning, uh"—she squinted at the name tag on his lapel—"Mr. Barnes. Do I need to buy a ticket?"

"No charge," said Mr. Barnes. "When your great-grandparents donated the building, they also donated money to sustain operations."

"I didn't know they donated the building," Effie said.

"Oh my, yes." Mr. Barnes was a young man with light hair. He spoke fast and moved with birdlike quickness. "Mr. Zook was a great man, a wonderful civic booster, and very generous. Are you here to learn more about him?"

"And my great-grandmother, too," said Effie, "but I'm sure the other exhibits are also excellent."

"They are," Mr. Barnes agreed, "but the average person is more interested in the inventor of the barf—that is, the *emesis*—bag than in the regional history of alfalfa production. I assume you already know the basics of your family story?"

"I know Gus Zook was a great man," said Effie, "and his wife was kind. And I know that because of his patent on the invention, my mom and my Aunt Clare get 1.7 cents for every emesis bag that's ever sold."

Mr. Barnes's eyebrows shot up. "Why, there must be millions of emesis bags sold!"

"Many millions," Effie agreed. "And I have a question if it's okay. Do you know anything about bad blood between the Zook family and the Yoders? Bad blood means something bad happened a long time ago and everybody is still mad. Since this is a museum, I thought you might have 'long time ago' covered."

Mr. Barnes frowned thoughtfully, then shook his head. "No, I don't," he said. "And frankly, bad blood would surprise me. You may not realize what an admirer Rob Yoder is of your great-grandfather. He's delved into our Zookiana archive more than once."

"Zookiana?" Effie repeated.

"By that I mean Mr. Zook's papers and effects," Mr. Barnes explained. "We have the world's most comprehensive collection—even if there is a gap in the record."

"A gap? What do you mean?"

"Sadly, we don't have a lot from Mr. Zook's later years," Mr. Barnes said. "It happens. The family doesn't recognize the historic significance of a piece of paper or photo; things are lost or thrown away. We in the museum game are used to it."

"I'm sorry," said Effie.

"I am too," said Mr. Barnes, "but rather than getting maudlin over what we lack, let's focus on what we have. If you like, I could give you the same speech I give to the school groups. Then you can tour the exhibit on your own."

"I would like that," Effie said. "Thank you."

Mr. Barnes stood up straight and looked over Effie's head as if a crowd were in the room behind her. "Can you hear me all right?" he asked.

"Just fine," said Effie.

Mr. Barnes cleared his throat. "Gustavus 'Gus' Zook was born in 1910 and grew up at nearby Zook Farm, which is still in the family and still a going agricultural concern. As a boy, Gus displayed a talent for engineering, and in time he left this rural redoubt for the bright lights of Pittsburgh and its educational opportunities. In college there he met Effie Tsikitas, who would become his wife.

"Gus Zook's young manhood coincided with the early days of commercial aviation. As he climbed the career ladder in his chosen field of engineering, this self-described country boy availed himself on numerous occasions of this innovative and efficient mode of transportation. Each time he did so, he discovered to his dismay the unfortunate consequences of having been born with a delicate stomach.

"Gus Zook was only twenty-six years of age when he took sharpened pencil to paper and drew the specs for a safe, sanitary, inexpensive, and compact container that would lessen the sufferings of air passengers such as himself—a safe, sanitary, inexpensive, and compact container that would become, with further refinements, the emesis bag all of us know and love today."

At this point Mr. Barnes, obviously awed and humbled by Gus Zook's achievement, paused and bowed his head. Effie, who had been to plenty of Broadway shows, recognized the cue and applauded.

Mr. Barnes raised his eyes and looked to the far distance. "Thank you," he said earnestly. "The rest, as they say in academe, is history. Enjoy your visit today. Donations are gratefully accepted. Please feel free to visit the gift shop conveniently located to the rear of the building by the restrooms."

"Oh, wow—there's a gift shop?" said Effie.

"It's really just a rack of postcards," Mr. Barnes

confided. "My particular favorite shows the original plans for the emesis bag. Twenty-five cents, or five for a dollar. Now, if you don't mind, I'll go back to working on my project upstairs. Call if you need me."

Effie thanked Mr. Barnes again, took a breath, and went through the doorway to the Zook Room. There seemed to be butterflies contending in her stomach. Maybe now she would get answers.

CHAPTER
19

The Zook Room was dominated by a portrait of Gustavus Zook himself staring down from over the fireplace. In the picture, the great man leaned against a fence with his arms crossed over his chest. There were black goats in the background. He was dressed in a blue work shirt, jeans, and boots.

Effie had never seen this painting and studied it for a moment. Her great-grandfather had had the same round blue eyes as her mother and aunt, the same apple cheeks and square face.

More striking than any of that, though, was his abundant, light brown beard. Effie couldn't help but think of Rob Yoder. Did her great-grandfather resemble him? Or was it only that they had similar beards?

Effie sighed and shook her head. *This is not good,* she thought. *I have more questions now than I did before.*

In the middle of the room were a settee and chairs, uncomfortable like the ones in the parlor at Zook Farm. On either side of the fireplace were bookcases. Along the window wall and the one opposite were four glass display cases. Framed pictures, paintings, and maps hung here and there, some labeled and some not.

Posted at intervals on the walls were text panels, each one telling a portion of Gustavus Zook's life story. The information on the first one, "Childhood," was familiar. Gus was an only child, his parents had farmed, his father had had a knack for machinery and eventually opened the town's first garage and auto repair shop.

In the first display case were white leather baby shoes, an embroidered christening gown, a faded certificate for good citizenship from Penn Creek Elementary School, and two handwritten report cards, one from second grade and one from fifth. Gus

Zook's grades, Effie noticed, were no better than her own—and she wasn't even a genius inventor!

Between the report cards lay a class picture. Effie counted eighteen kids in two rows standing solemnly on the steps in front of the school. They looked to be about Effie's age, maybe fifth or sixth grade. Bangs were popular. The girls and the teachers all wore dark dresses; the boys wore jackets and white shirts. Gus Zook was identified by a white arrow drawn on the glass protecting the picture.

To Effie the kids all looked similar except for one, the girl standing next to Gus Zook. She was black.

Maybe that's Mr. Odbody's grandmother, Effie thought, *Sadie Pendleton. Has Mr. Odbody been here? Has he seen this picture?*

Also in the case were front pages from the local newspaper. The one from 1917, when Gus had been in second grade, was headlined US ENTERS THE WAR ON SIDE OF ALLIES. The one from 1918 said KAISER SURRENDERS!

The last thing in the case was a well-worn mitt displayed with a newspaper page. The headline read, PENN CREEK FLASH ON FIRE! The article began, *The Red*

Flash crushed Bellefonte last night in a 7–0 rout that also saw standout pitcher Gus Zook come within a fare-thee-well of a no-hitter.

Effie grinned. *I guess I inherited my throwing arm from Gus Zook,* she thought, *even if my looks all come from Effie.*

Effie was moving on to the next display case when she heard the front door open, then the *ding* of the call bell.

"Holy crumb! More company!" said Mr. Barnes as he came down the stairs.

Effie took a step back and looked into the entry hall. "Hey!" she said, all smiles. "What are you doing here?"

Moriah smiled back. "Same as you."

CHAPTER

20

Moriah's mom had a dentist appointment. Moriah had talked her into a trip to town. When Moriah found that Sadie's was closed, she had tried to think where Effie might go. There weren't many places in Penn Creek where a kid could hang out. She had checked the diner first and then the museum.

"Do you know what happened to Sadie's?" Effie asked.

"I was hoping you did," Moriah said.

"So I take it you girls know each other," said Mr. Barnes. "And I believe you're Mr. Yoder's daughter? I had the pleasure of talking to him at Fourthfest.

He's a friend of the museum, you know."

"He is?" Moriah said.

"Oh my, yes. He has such good suggestions. I assume you've been here before, Moriah?"

"Field trips," said Moriah.

"Then you've certainly heard my little talk. Would you mind terribly if I went back to work upstairs? We have funding for a new exhibit: 'Men's Grooming in Pennsylvania, Early Trends.'"

The girls said they'd be fine on their own, and Mr. Barnes left them.

In the Zook Room, Moriah asked, "Why do you think Sadie's closed all of a sudden?"

"I hardly want to think about it," Effie said. "Now what will I do all day? Also, I'm worried about Mr. Odbody."

"Why?" Moriah said.

Effie told her how Chop Suey was still at the store. "So Mr. Odbody left in a hurry," Effie said. "And it's crazy, but yesterday I told my aunt and uncle that I'd been hanging out at Sadie's. Did they cancel his lease, do you think? Did they do it all of a sudden because they found out I was going there?"

"That can't be right," Moriah said.

Effie shook her head. "Another question I can't answer."

Moriah's eyes were drawn to the big portrait. "Your great-grandfather's beard is like my pa's," she said.

Effie nodded. "I noticed that," she said. "I like it here, do you? The old-timey-ness is interesting, the newspapers and stuff. I guess I like history."

"Me too," Moriah said. "What answers are you looking for exactly?"

"Clues," said Effie. "At Fourthfest Mrs. McMinty said something about legal drama. Does it have anything to do with what happened between our families, the bad blood? The grown-ups are keeping secrets, Moriah. I want to find out what."

Moriah knit her brows. "Maybe it's something we kids shouldn't know, Effie. Papa says—"

"I know all about what your papa says," Effie interrupted. "He thinks kids have mush for brains. But he's wrong, Moriah. Kids should ask questions. We deserve answers, just like anybody else."

Effie hadn't meant to be rude, but Moriah made a face like she'd been slapped.

Oh, no—she's going to cry! Effie thought, and got ready to apologize, but before she could, Moriah got mad. "You're from New York City, and you have rich, famous parents, Effie, and I'm just some kid who lives on a farm. But I'm as good as you, and my pa is plenty smart, and I don't have to be your friend if I don't want to."

Effie said, "Moriah . . . ," not knowing exactly how the rest of the sentence was supposed to go. The way it turned out, it didn't matter. Moriah turned her back and headed out of the Zook Room and out the museum's front door.

Effie was left all alone, breathing hard and feeling slapped herself.

Who wants her around anyway? she thought, trying to calm down. *She and I could never be real friends. We're too different. Her family's too crazy.*

The museum door closed with a click, and Moriah was really gone. *Anyway, I don't have time for friends,* Effie thought, wiping her eyes. *I am much too busy.*

As if to prove it, she stared back into the display case. For several moments, though, the items she was looking at refused to make sense. It was easy to say you didn't care and you didn't need friends. It was hard to make yourself feel that way.

At last, though, Effie's brain allowed itself to be distracted. There in front of her were Gus and Effie's caps from college graduation, their wedding notice from the *Pine Creek Weekly*, and a California picture postcard, propped up so both sides were visible.

The photo was an orange blossom. Effie had to walk around the case to read the note on the back, handwritten in small, precise print: *Dear Ma & Pa, The weather is always beautiful here, and the orange blossoms on the trees smell nice. But it ain't home! Warm regards from Effie. Love, Gus.*

Grandpa Bob's birth certificate from Good Samaritan Hospital in Los Angeles was also in the case. Robert Gustavus Zook had been born at 6:11 a.m. on December 1, 1939. He had weighed seven pounds, six ounces, a pound less than Effie herself.

Later, he made up for it with all those seafood platters, Effie thought.

The newspaper headlines were about bread-lines and bank runs, migrants from the dust bowl, the German army in Czechoslovakia. There were photos of Franklin and Eleanor Roosevelt.

Framed on the wall behind the case was a drawing of a barf bag, including dimensions and manufacturing specifications. Effie remembered what Mr. Barnes had said about Gus Zook's sharpened pencil. The round, loopy writing was faded but legible. Included was the chemical formula for a "vulcanized water-repellant coating."

On the wall next to the sketch was a printed museum label: *This is the original design for the emesis bag, sketched when Gustavus Zook was a resident of Los Angeles, California, and later patented by him.*

The great man's life story continued on the next panel: *World War II saw dramatically increased demand for emesis bags to ensure the comfort, hygiene, convenience, and safety of thousands of Allied airmen. While Mr. Zook occasionally expressed disappointment that none of his other inventions were enjoying comparable success, he took heart in knowing his work had made a special contribution to the Allied victory.*

A photo in the third display case showed Gus, Effie, and Robert smiling beside a big black car in the driveway of this very house. A later photo, dated 1950, showed the family in the driveway of the pretty yellow farmhouse. Father and son were smiling, but Effie the First was not. In fact, she wasn't even looking at the camera. She was looking to her left, toward what was now Moriah's house, as if a noise in that direction had disturbed her.

I wonder if maybe she heard Boris's great-great-great-great-great-grandfather barking, Effie thought. *I wonder if something was after her goats.*

The final display case contained mementos of her great-grandparents' good works in Penn Creek: scissors from the ribbon-cutting that opened the new museum; a test tube from the new science lab for the high school; ribbons from county fair 4-H Club auctions. It seemed that Effie's great-grandmother had bought more than her share of prize-winning goats.

By this time Effie had read a lot and seen a lot. All of it—not to mention Sadie's being closed and Moriah being angry—made her head spin. There might be clues right in front of her nose, but at the moment she was too stupid to decipher them. *You have to forget*

Moriah and forget Sadie's, she told herself. *You have to think!*

The fifth panel of Gus Zook's life story began: *Gustavus Zook approached the personal, political, and societal challenges of the late 1960s and the 1970s with characteristic flexibility of mind, creativity, and goodwill. Sadly, many of his ideas were so far ahead of their time as to guarantee misunderstanding by those with lesser vision. Along with . . .*

And that is what Effie was reading when the sound of an opening door interrupted and she looked up. From where she was standing, she had only to turn her head to see the new visitor.

Uncle Ted?

"Oh, Effie, thank goodness!" he said. "I thought that was your bicycle. I've been looking everywhere." He waved her toward the door. "I have some news, but I don't want you to worry. Your aunt is setting up the Skype call. Everything"—his voice caught—"is going to be fine."

21

Effie hardly knew what she was doing as she walked outside and climbed into the truck. Her uncle got in. They fastened their seat belts. He started the truck and steered it out of the parking lot. Effie didn't trust her voice to speak until they were on the Penn Creek Bridge.

"What happened? Are my parents all right?"

"How about," her uncle said hopefully, "if we let your aunt explain when we get home?"

"I want you to explain now," Effie said. "Please."

The road hummed beneath the truck. Uncle Ted shifted in his seat, keeping his eyes straight ahead. "Something went wrong with the plane, and—"

Effie wanted to hear the rest, but she couldn't because somebody was crying. Only when Uncle Ted handed her a tissue did she realize she was the somebody. The second time through, the words sank in. Her mother had been flying when *Sunspot I* lost altitude over the Pacific. Her distress call was relayed to the US Navy. The nearest rescue vessel was on its way to the plane's last-known position.

"That does not sound good," Effie murmured.

"Your dad was able to monitor most of the descent," said Uncle Ted. "He told your aunt it was controlled. So that's a good thing."

"Where is Daddy?" Effie asked.

"En route from Japan to Honolulu," said Uncle Ted. "The signal was poor; that's why what Clare found out is a little muddled. When he lands, I'm sure he'll Skype so he can talk to you."

"How soon?" Effie asked.

"Soon," said her uncle.

Aunt Clare was standing on the front porch as the truck came up the driveway. She ran out and met them by the garage. Boris was there too, wagging his tail and dancing in happy, welcoming circles.

"Effie, I'm so sorry, but it's all going to be okay—you'll see—," Aunt Clare began at the same time Boris jumped up and put his big dirty paws on Effie's shoulders, causing her to stagger and step back. Boris was a smelly, grimy outdoor dog whose bed was in the barn. He had no manners. But at least he was honest.

"The only truthful one around is Boris!" Effie snapped. "What is the matter with you? My mom might be dead, and you keep saying it'll be all right. Well, dead is not all right!"

"She's not dead," said Aunt Clare.

"Is there news?" Uncle Ted asked.

"No, uh . . . that is, no," said Aunt Clare.

Effie snorted. Her aunt didn't know anything. None of them knew anything. "So how do we get news?" Effie asked.

"I've got my iPad right here." Aunt Clare held it up. "I'm just waiting for your dad to Skype. Come on inside. We will get some tea or juice or something."

Effie didn't want tea or juice. Effie didn't want anything except for time to pass so her dad would call. Not knowing was awful. But if the news was bad news, the worst possible news, news you couldn't take back or make better, then knowing would be worse.

Wouldn't it?

Since she couldn't sit still, Effie paced—from the kitchen to the dining room through the front hall to the parlor to the sunroom around the back stairs and into the kitchen again. Her aunt and uncle stayed put at the kitchen table. She knew she was driving them crazy, and she didn't care.

She tried to think logically, as if logic would provide the tape and string to hold her together. *My mother is a good pilot.* Sunspot *carried a life raft. The United States Navy has good sailors and good ships. She was wearing a helmet. There are sharks in the ocean. How fast did the plane descend? Why hasn't my dad called yet? My mother is a good pilot. She was wearing a helmet.*

If Effie could stick to logic, she wouldn't think about living in a big house in Brooklyn with only her father, and she wouldn't think about happy times with her mom, either—looking at the Manhattan skyline together, looking at old photo albums, her mom reading to her before bed, the night her mom came back from a long trip and woke Effie up to look at the sunrise and eat ice cream for breakfast.

Effie's mom was not reliable. She did not volunteer at school. She did not remember the rule about no peanuts. She forgot to send birthday party invitations. But she loved Effie. Effie had never doubted it.

And she had promised she would come back.

Effie's thoughts were zigzagging on unproductive paths when her phone chirped. It was in her pocket. Familiar as the ringtone was, Effie couldn't place the cricket sound for several moments. Then she remembered: Jasmine.

"Hello?"

"Effie, hello—is your mom okay? Alice just heard on the news!" Alice was Jasmine's family's nanny.

"It's on the news?" Effie hadn't thought of that.

"Alice says so. Not the first story or anything. How are you? How is your mom?"

"I don't know," Effie said.

"You don't know how you are, or you don't know how your mom is?"

Jasmine's questions could make a person crazy, but right now Effie liked the reminder that some stuff in the world remained normal. "Both," she said. "Dad's supposed to call."

"Oh, golly, I feel bad for you," said Jasmine. "If *my* mom were dead, I—"

"She's not dead!" said Effie.

"Not dead," said Jasmine quickly. "But if she's dead—"

"Jasmine!"

"Sorry, okay, sorry," said Jasmine. "Nothing this bad has ever happened to me—"

"It still hasn't. It's happening to *me*," said Effie.

"I know," Jasmine said, "and it's awful, and I don't know what I'm supposed to say. What am I supposed to say?"

Effie's pacing had brought her back to the parlor, where she realized her knees were weak. She dropped down onto the old, uncomfortable settee. "I don't know either," she said.

"Will you call me when you find out more?" Jasmine asked.

"No," said Effie.

"But you are my best friend!" Jasmine whined.

"I know," said Effie. "I might call. It depends."

"On if she's dead?" Jasmine said.

"On how I feel about stuff," Effie said, "on whether I want to talk, on whether I want to talk to *you*."

"Are you still my best friend?" Jasmine asked.

"Yes," Effie said, "but that's not what I'm thinking about right now."

"You're thinking about your mom," said Jasmine.

"Yes," said Effie. "Good-bye, Jasmine."

She hung up and went into the kitchen, where her aunt and uncle were sitting at the kitchen table. "We should turn on the news," Effie said.

"Is that a good idea?" Uncle Ted asked. "The media isn't always reliable."

"Can we please turn on the news?" Effie repeated. Her aunt reached for the remote at the same time that the Skype tone on the iPad rang.

CHAPTER

22

Effie's father was standing outdoors in the open, with a line of palm trees and the clear sky behind him. It was eight a.m. in Hawaii. On the screen, her father's face was at a funny angle, and he looked tired, but Effie focused on one thing. When her father was upset, a furrow dug itself between his eyebrows. There was no furrow now. That was how Effie knew what he was going to say before he spoke, and relief surged through her.

"Mom's all right, isn't she?"

Her father nodded, choked up, and at last managed three words: "Yes. She's okay."

Everybody cried. Then Effie hugged her aunt and

uncle and apologized for being rude, horrid, and ungrateful. They said that was okay. She wished more than anything that she was hugging her dad and her mom, too. It was a while before anyone could speak, and as soon as they could, the Skype connection broke. A long half hour of interrupted explanation passed before Effie understood what had happened.

It was the solar batteries, her father said. They had stopped giving consistent power to the propellers, and because of that the plane lost altitude. There were no airfields nearby, no islands, no place to land. Effie's mom had been forced to ditch in the Pacific.

"In the end, the propellers completely shut down, but Molly kept the plane under control," her father said. "It skimmed along the whitecaps, then finally settled down onto the surface."

"How do you know all this?" Aunt Clare asked.

"I monitored her descent by satellite. Then, once she was safely in the life raft, I talked to her on the emergency radio."

"So now," said Uncle Ted, "I suppose you'll be in Hawaii for a while, overseeing the investigation. You'll want to know exactly what went wrong."

"Actually . . . , no," said Effie's father. "We won't be staying long. The navy will bring Molly to port with all deliberate speed. We'll fly back as soon as we can secure transportation."

Effie couldn't wait to see her parents, to touch them and be certain for herself that they were okay. But a tiny part of her was disappointed, too. She wanted to uncover the family secret. She had thought she had all summer to do it, but now she'd be going back to Brooklyn. Once she was home, would she ever find out the truth?

"I don't understand," Aunt Clare was saying. "Aren't you going to take the plane apart? Dissect those batteries?"

"We do want to investigate," said Effie's dad, "for the sake of science and engineering and the future of aviation. But right now further study isn't, uh . . . practical. The plane seems to have survived the water landing pretty well. But once Molly was safely in the life raft, it sank. Right now, as far as we know, it's under fifteen thousand feet of ocean."

"Oh dear," said Aunt Clare.

"But you'll raise her?" said Uncle Ted.

"Not anytime soon," said Effie's father. "There are, uh . . . certain financial exigencies."

"I don't understand," said Effie.

"Oh dear," said Aunt Clare, and Effie noticed that she and her uncle had turned pale.

What was the matter with them, anyway? Effie was sad for her parents too, but all of them had known the trip was risky. And it wasn't Aunt Clare and Uncle Ted's airplane at the bottom of the ocean.

"Leaving all that aside for now," said Effie's dad, "I think you'd better prepare for an influx of media on your end."

"Oh dear," said Aunt Clare.

"Yes, well, it can't be helped," said Effie's father. "What if you recruited a family spokesman?"

At this suggestion, Aunt Clare perked up. "I know just the person," she said.

"You do?" Uncle Ted looked at her.

Aunt Clare nodded firmly and reached for her phone. "I do, and she will love taking her rightful place smack-dab in the middle of the action."

23

The family is, of course, disappointed by the abrupt end to the pioneering mission and the loss of the experimental aircraft. We are heartened, however, by the outpouring of support from friends around the world. Most important, we are relieved beyond measure that brave Molly Zook—scion of Penn Creek's most prominent family—is safely aboard a US Navy destroyer bound for the Hawaiian Islands."

As Aunt Clare had anticipated, Mrs. McMinty had been more than happy to step up and represent the family before the media. In her eagerness to answer Aunt Clare's call, she had broken every speed limit in the county. Now, having read aloud the statement hastily written by Aunt Clare and Uncle Ted, she stood on the front porch, magisterially regarding the TV trucks and reporters spread out before her.

Her lipstick, applied more carefully than usual, was pink to match her T-shirt. In deference to the seriousness of the occasion, she wore baggy capri pants in place of her usual baggy shorts.

Hunkered down in the parlor with the blinds drawn, Aunt Clare, Uncle Ted, and Effie could hear everything said outside.

"Any questions?" Mrs. McMinty asked, and Aunt Clare squealed: "No-o-o-o! She is supposed to say, 'Thank you for respecting the family's privacy, and good afternoon.'"

"I don't get it," Effie said. "She doesn't know anything else. How is she going to answer questions?"

"Not knowing anything won't stop her," said Uncle Ted, and he was right.

Mrs. McMinty was in her element. The reporters went bananas trying to get her attention, and one by one she called on them.

When the guy from WNEP wanted to know how

Effie had taken the news about her mother, Mrs. McMinty told a long story about how she herself had taken the news of her late husband's first heart attack.

A lady from WPGH asked if the loss of the plane would set back solar aviation, and she told an even longer story about the time her neighbor's rooster flew the coop.

"What does that have to do with anything?" yelled reporter Tapper Sprocket of the *Harrisburg Patriot-News*.

"I think," Mrs. McMinty sniffed, "that the message is clear to anyone glancingly familiar with American history."

The questions continued, as did the chatty, irrelevant answers. Finally, Uncle Ted peered out from between the slats of the window blinds. "Some of them are starting to pack up," he reported.

"She wore them down!" said Aunt Clare with satisfaction.

"That woman," said Uncle Ted, "is a genius."

Only after Effie had turned out her light that night did she think of Sadie's and realize she should have asked Mrs. McMinty if she knew what was going on. There had been plenty of time for that, too. After the widow's triumphant performance as family spokesperson, she had come into the parlor to enjoy hors d'oeuvres and admiration. But Effie hadn't said a word about the bookstore or Mr. Odbody either. The abrupt conclusion to *Sunspot I*'s mission had wiped them clean out of her head.

Effie's next thought made her sit up in bed. *What about Chop Suey?*

She pulled her phone over and saw that it was almost ten o'clock. Her uncle was probably asleep, tired out after an emotion-packed day. Also, he and her aunt had to drive all the way to Johnstown for an appointment the next morning. Effie had asked if she could go too, but they had told her it would be every kind of grown-up boring.

Chop Suey has food and water, Effie reminded herself. *If Uncle Ted can't take me, I'll think of a way to bring him home myself.*

Effie slept well that night in spite of the thoughts doing battle in her head.

Elsewhere, other people were not so successful.

Moriah, for example, tossed and turned. As soon as she had heard about Effie's mom, she felt terrible she'd gotten angry at her friend. The truth was Moriah sometimes questioned her pa's wisdom too. For that matter, so did her mom.

You had to be loyal to family, though. That was Precept 12, besides being plain old natural. When someone outside the family, someone like Effie, questioned Pa's wisdom, what could she do but defend him?

Still, pitching a fit hadn't been necessary. She wished she had talked to Effie about it. Now that her parents' trip was over, they would come for their daughter, and she would go home. Moriah wondered if she would ever see Effie again.

Seven time zones away, aboard the *USS Higgins*, Effie's mother was supposed to be resting. But resting was not really the word for what she was doing. The word for it was crying.

Alone in the destroyer's sick bay, Molly Zook cried for all kinds of reasons. She was heartbroken she had lost *Sunspot I*. She was upset that she had almost died. She was grateful that she had not died. She missed her daughter.

And there was one more reason too.

Molly Zook was anxious. When *Sunspot I* sank, it took with it the best hope for saving the Zook family fortune. All of them had counted on the airplane's success creating a demand for its patented solar technology. They would sell it and be rich again. But now *Sunspot I* was at the bottom of the Pacific and, as of tomorrow, the family would more than likely be broke.

Molly didn't think she would enjoy being poor. If she had to get a job, what would she do? She had a pilot's license. If she learned to fly helicopters, she could ferry her friends around. A lot of them had beach houses with guest rooms. Maybe they'd let her stay over sometimes.

Molly blinked to clear the tears and then rolled over. Before her eyes was a map of the world that someone had affixed to the bulkhead. Molly propped herself up on an elbow and found Pennsylvania. Penn Creek was too small to be marked, but she knew where it was. Her daughter was there.

The state capital, Harrisburg, was eighty miles southeast, and marked by a star. There in the offices of the *Patriot-News*, reporter Tapper Sprocket was at that moment tapping at the keyboard on her desk.

Molly had never heard of Tapper Sprocket, but the young reporter knew all about Molly. In fact, she had been investigating the Zook family for two years, ever since a challenge to Gustavus Zook's will was filed in the Cambria County Court of Common Pleas.

Tapper couldn't finish that story until the judge made her decision, and—like most of the parties to the case—she would be on hand in the courtroom in the Cambria County seat, Johnstown, the next morning.

Now, though, the untimely end to Molly Zook's round-the-world flight meant she had to rush something into print right away.

"We need a bulletin for the Web in half an hour," the state editor told her. "And the rest by eleven for the morning edition. We can't beat the TV, but you got the depth, right? You've been reporting this story long enough."

"Depth I got," said Tapper, and for the first time all day she smiled. She was thinking of the strange, blind creatures that lived in the depths of the Pacific Ocean. How surprised they must have been when *Sunspot I* drifted gently down to join them.

CHAPTER

24

By the time Effie came downstairs the next morning, Aunt Clare and Uncle Ted had left for their appointment in Johnstown. It wasn't that far, they told her, but the rural roads were narrow and winding. It would take a big chunk of the day to get there and back.

Facing hours by herself with nothing to do, Effie went outside and greeted Alfred (who ignored her) and Boris (who went crazy with joy). She could hear a tractor out back. With Uncle Ted away, one of the hired guys was getting a field ready for planting.

It seemed like a lifetime ago that Effie had tried and failed to go to the diner for breakfast. The owners must be back from vacation by now. She would eat a Greek omelet and rye toast. She would figure out how in the world she could rescue Chop Suey without anyone to drive her. She would find out the meaning of the sign that said THE ALPHA AND OMEGA OF PENN CREEK.

The bike ride to town had become routine. She barely noticed the trees, mailboxes, driveways, and houses whizzing by. A big truck passed and she didn't flinch. Soon she had crossed the bridge and sailed down Main Street to arrive at her destination.

Inside the diner, the blast of AC gave Effie goose bumps. When she looked around, she saw she was in a comfortable, bright place with wood paneling and orange tabletops. The waitress behind the counter was wearing a checkered uniform. Effie had been to plenty of diners in New York; the waitresses never wore uniforms.

"Table for one?" the waitress asked. She was wiry and energetic-looking with straight brown hair. "Or would you rather sit at the counter?"

"Counter, please." Effie liked sitting high up on a stool.

"Take a seat." The waitress's name tag said TERRY. "Can I get you some coffee?"

"Yes, please."

Effie looked at the menu, then looked up. There was no TV. Only two tables had customers. She wished she had brought a book. She was almost done with the fourth volume of The Exiles. With Sadie's out of business, where would she get something new to read? She saw a newspaper at the other end of the counter. She pulled it toward her and was astonished to see her mother was on the front page.

Molly Z Survives Crash Landing in Pacific
SOLAR PLANE SINKS, ENDING ROUND-THE-WORLD QUEST

Effie skimmed the story, most of it exactly what her father had said the day before, plus the statement from Mrs. McMinty—old news. Then Effie turned the page to where the story was continued:

The loss of the experimental plane on top of the loss of sponsor backing for the pioneering round-the-world expedition will in all likelihood deal a

crushing blow to the Zook family fortune, accord-
ing to information amassed in an ongoing investi-
gation by the Patriot-News.

A complaint due to be adjudicated today,
Wednesday, in the Cambria County Court of
Common Pleas offers compelling evidence that
Gustavus Zook's estate should have been divided
among three surviving children rather than the one
child known to the court at the time of the demise
of the widow of the inventor-philanthropist.

The estate includes property in and around
Penn Creek as well as vast revenue generated by
Mr. Zook's patents. If the new findings are deemed
relevant and upheld, the scions of the original heir,
Robert Zook, who died in Boca Raton, Fla., in 2010,
could be ordered to pay to claimants a two-thirds
share of all monies derived from those patents dat-
ing back to Mr. Zook's widow's death in 1983.

The judgment could also result in the transfer,
sale, or liquidation of substantial real property in
and around Penn Creek, with untold but in all like-
lihood profound effects on the small community's
character and economic well-being.

Effie read the article twice. When she looked up after the second time, she was surprised to see that there was an omelet in front of her along with toast and coffee. She put her napkin in her lap, picked up her fork, took a bite of the omelet, and swallowed. She buttered the toast. She sipped the coffee.

But she didn't taste a thing.

She wished she read newspaper stories more often. The writing style and some of the words confused her. But she thought she got the idea. When *Sunspot I* sank, the people and companies that had helped pay for the trip decided not to pay anymore. So that explained why her dad and mom weren't going to stay in Hawaii to find out what went wrong. There wasn't enough money.

That was the first part of the story; the second part was even more amazing.

Somebody was claiming that Effie's great-grandfather didn't have only one child—her Grandpa Bob—he had three children. The case was being decided today, at this very moment maybe. If the judge said so, her family was going to have to pay back most of the money and property her great-grandparents had left to them. Plus they'd have to pay back most of the barf bag money, past and future.

Effie did the math in her head. Instead of 1.7 cents per barf bag, her mom would now earn roughly half a cent.

We're broke, Effie thought.

But even that wasn't the most amazing part.

This was: If the story was right, her grandfather had siblings no one had ever told her about. Why hadn't they told her? Why weren't there photos somewhere? There were family photos at her house. There were family photos at the museum. But there were no photos of children except for her grandfather.

Maybe there was something wrong with the other children, Effie thought. *Maybe they were sick, or crazy, or criminals.*

"How's everything taste?" Terry appeared on the other side of the counter.

Effie blinked. "What?"

"You okay, honey? You look a little piqued, if you don't mind my saying so."

"I'm fine," Effie said. "Sorry. The omelet's good. I'm just—"

"Reading about your mom, huh?" Terry had glanced down at the newspaper. "I haven't taken a look at this yet, but I hear she's unhurt."

As often as it had happened in Penn Creek, being recognized still surprised Effie sometimes. "Oh, so you know who I am too," she said.

"Sure I do, hon. Us Greeks gotta stick together."

"I am one-eighth Greek," Effie said.

"Same here," said Terry. "And you look it more than me, if you don't mind my saying so. All that beautiful black hair."

"Do you think it's beautiful?" Effie tugged a curl by her ear.

"Oh yeah." Terry nodded. "My own hair's blah and no color at all. What I wouldn't give to have yours."

"Thank you," Effie said. "I mean, not that your hair isn't perfectly nice because it is. May I ask you a question? Do other people around here know about this? Not the airplane part, but about my great-grandparents' money?"

"It could be that some people knew before today," Terry said, "but not me. See, the complaint wasn't filed in the local court. It was filed in Cambria County.

I don't think anyone around here pays attention to filings out of town. That was smart on somebody's part, keep it quiet as long as possible."

"Where is Cambria County?" Effie asked.

"Maybe seventy miles south?" said Terry. "The county seat is Johnstown."

Effie felt her heart skip. "My aunt and uncle are there right now!"

"Stands to reason, hon," said Terry. "They're probably having their day in court right along with the plaintiffs."

"Plaintiffs? What does that mean?" Effie asked.

"The people who are complaining," said Terry. "In other words, whoever it is that claims they're kin to your great-grandpa and wants a share of the money."

Effie breathed in and out. So the mystery children, grown up by now, were in Johnstown today too.

"Can I ask you one more question?" Effie said.

"Sure, hon. Shoot," said Terry.

"How come the diner is 'the Alpha and Omega of Penn Creek'?"

Terry nodded. "I get that one a lot. Alpha and

omega are the first and last letters of the Greek alphabet, right? So if you're coming into town from the south, the diner's the first thing you come to, the alpha. And if you're leaving town from the north, it's the last thing you leave, the omega."

"Finally I've asked a question with an answer," Effie said.

"May it be the beginning of a trend," said Terry.

Effie left the rest of her omelet, which had turned rubbery by this time, and finished the coffee. Terry offered her more, but she declined and asked for the check. When Terry brought it, she remembered she had one more question.

"Sure, hon. Let's see if we can go two for two," said Terry.

"Is there a place in town I can buy a cat carrier?"

"You know what?" Terry laughed. "That is not a question I was expecting."

Effie laughed too, and laughing felt good. "I guess it wasn't," she said, and then she explained about Chop Suey. Terry thought it was a shame that the only bookstore for miles around had closed. And she was a cat lover herself.

"Tell you what," she said. "Another girl comes

in to take care of lunch. I'll be off in about an hour. If you can wait till then, I can give you a hand with the kitty. Shouldn't take long to run you both to Zook Farm."

CHAPTER
25

With an hour to kill, Effie's destination was obvious. Soon she was leaning her bike against the steps at the Museum of the Town of Penn Creek. She had done exactly the same thing the day before—before *Sunspot I* went down, before the family secrets started to spill.

Inside, she rang the call bell and—what the heck—signed the guest book again. Soon Mr. Barnes came tripping down the stairs, smiling and happy to see her. "Welcome, welcome. The men's grooming exhibit is coming along very well, in case you were wondering. Did you know Chester Arthur's election in 1880 started a Pennsylvania-wide fad for muttonchop whiskers? Oh—and I was so glad to hear that your mother is all right."

"I didn't know that about whiskers," said Effie. "And I'm glad about my mother too."

She noticed that there was stubble on Mr. Barnes's face, as if he hadn't been shaving. He must have seen her look because he rubbed his chin. "They tell me that the itching goes away."

"I'm sure you'll look very handsome with a beard," Effie said.

"Thank you," said Mr. Barnes. "Your great-grandfather, of course, believed that men should grow beards, that a beard was an emblem of manly vigor."

"That must be where BFA got the idea," Effie said.

"I believe so," said Mr. Barnes.

"Are you growing a beard because of BFA? Did you join?" Effie asked.

Mr. Barnes didn't answer directly. "As I mentioned yesterday, Mr. Yoder is a great friend of the museum. And I can't deny that some of BFA's precepts are appealing. I'll certainly be supporting him in his run for mayor."

"Mr. Barnes," said Effie patiently, "no offense to

you or to Moriah, but those guys are crackpots."

Mr. Barnes was not a tall man, but he was taller than Effie, and now he drew himself up to full height. "Crackpots?" he repeated. "Or visionaries ahead of their time, same as your great-grandfather was?"

"The barf bag was visionary?" Effie said doubtfully.

"Sure it was," said Mr. Barnes, "and so were his many other inventions."

Effie was as fond of the barf bag as anyone, but she thought "visionary" might be an exaggeration. "What were his other visionary inventions?" she asked.

Mr. Barnes hesitated. "Well, here's the thing. Do you remember my telling you yesterday how there is a gap in the record? You see, it's because of that gap that his later inventions largely remain obscure."

Now Effie was confused. "So how do you know they ever existed?" she asked. "And if you do know they existed, how do you know they were visionary, et cetera?"

Mr. Barnes sighed. "You ask a lot of questions."

Effie nodded. "I do. It's the way I learn stuff. And Gus Zook was a great man, I guess, but it sounds to me like he might have had some crackpot ideas too."

Mr. Barnes looked horrified. "I wouldn't say that too loudly if I were you."

"I'm just trying to get at the truth," Effie said. "And I have another question. Did you talk to this person?" Effie pointed at the guest book entry from Saturday. "I can't read the name, but the initials look like 'T.S.', and whoever it is is from Harrisburg."

Mr. Barnes shook his head. "Not me. I wasn't here over the weekend."

Effie was disappointed. As of this morning, she thought she might know who this T.S. person was, and he (or she?) just might have some answers—but that would have to wait. "Okay. Last one—I promise," Effie said. "Did you know that if Mr. Yoder gets to be mayor, he wants to put foot-washing stations in every business?"

Mr. Barnes frowned. "He does?"

"Unh-hunh," Effie said. "And I can picture a school group right here on the floor, washing their feet before the tour. There will definitely be some splashing—you know how kids are. You might have to shorten your talk."

"I'll have to think about that one," said Mr. Barnes. "And now if you'll excuse me?"

"I know you have to get back to Grooming Trends," said Effie. "I don't have much time either."

Back in the Zook Room, Effie studied the portrait over the fireplace. Her great-grandmother had not yet spoken to her from her silver frame. Would her great-grandfather speak to her now?

"So what's the deep, dark family secret?" Effie asked out loud. "Why was my great-grandmother unhappy? Were there *three* children? What happened to the other two? For that matter, *who* were the other two? Oh, and while I've got your attention, what's all this about bad blood between Zooks and Yoders? Did that have anything to do with you?"

The smiling portrait only smiled. But maybe that was an answer too. Gus Zook had been a self-made man, no fortune behind him at all. And now there was no fortune behind Effie either. Maybe he was telling her to get to work.

Without much time, Effie decided to look first at what she'd missed the day before. She hoped she would be able to come back to the museum before going home to New York. Her parents were traveling such a long way. No chance they would arrive before next week.

The last Zook display case contained miscellaneous items. There were several varieties of barf bag, including a rainbow tie-dye edition from the late 1960s and one with yellow happy faces from the eighties. There were proclamations, medals, and newspaper clippings telling of Gus Zook's generosity and accomplishments. There was Grandpa Bob's diploma from Penn State.

What Effie really hoped for was a family photo that she hadn't noticed yesterday, one that included two mysterious unidentified children, but she found nothing like that. Instead there were photos similar to the ones her family had at home—Gus Zook with celebrities, generals, and politicians. On the wall behind the display case was a color photo of a wooden shack shaded by an elm tree. This photo had no label.

Effie checked her phone—almost time to meet Terry. Quickly, she read the final panel of Gustavus Zook's life story, the one entitled Legacy:

Gustavus Zook's declining years were marked by erratic behavior that may have been the result of failing health. This behavior sullied the reputation he deserved as a visionary. Thus, it is left to us, the living, to carry forward Zook's pioneering work and, in the fullness of time, to implement his plan for a better civilization, one that is at once more united, more hygienic, and more content.

Effie blinked. All her family ever said about Gus Zook was "great man," "great inventor." Nobody ever said anything about erratic behavior or a better civilization. Was this what BFA was about? A plan for the future based on her great-grandfather's ideas?

Now she had even more to think about.

Meanwhile, there was a cat to rescue.

Effie called good-bye to Mr. Barnes upstairs and headed for the door. Thinking back on what she'd just seen, she realized something. The shack in the color photo had looked kind of familiar.

Effie didn't want to be late. Terry was doing her a favor. But something made her return to take a closer look. The elm tree wasn't there anymore, but she knew that building. It stood at the far end of her aunt and uncle's driveway, about a quarter mile beyond the barn.

Effie slipped the picture off its hook and flipped it over. Written on the brown backing paper was a note in Gus Zook's small, precise print: *Workshop 1965, where the magic happens.*

Workshop? Effie thought.

That wasn't what Aunt Clare and Uncle Ted had called it. They had called it the shed.

And it was the one place at Zook Farm they had told her was off-limits.

26

At Zook Farm half an hour later, Effie waved good-bye to Terry and, dodging Boris all the way, carried Chop Suey into the yellow farmhouse and up the stairs to set him on her bed.

"Stay!" she commanded.

Chop Suey didn't.

Instead, he jumped from the bed to the lamp table, knocking one of Effie's books to the floor on the way. It was *Pippi Longstocking*. Effie bent down and grabbed the book, which opened to the flyleaf. There was the handwritten note from Effie the First to Aunt Clare: *May you always be as brave as Pippi.*

My mom is almost as brave as Pippi, Effie thought.

I'm not sure about Aunt Clare, though, or me either.

"You have to stay indoors," she told Chop Suey. "Boris acts all friendly, but you can't trust him. He'd turn you into chop suey for real if he got the chance."

The cat was uninterested in Effie's warnings, so Effie went downstairs to set up the litter box and food dishes. She was in the mudroom pouring out kitty chow when Chop Suey appeared beside her.

"Is this acceptable?" she asked the cat.

Chop Suey body-rubbed her shin and purred.

"Good," she said. "Time for my lunch now."

Effie fixed a peanut butter sandwich and poured a glass of milk. Then she sat down at the kitchen table to think.

Aunt Clare and Uncle Ted had dodged most of her questions. They had also told her to stay away from the shed. Was it really to protect her from falling towers of junk? From snakes and rats and opossums? Or was it because the shed held answers they didn't want her to have?

Thanks to Tapper Sprocket's story in the newspaper, Mrs. McMinty, the museum, and Terry, she was putting pieces together. Two people were suing her family to get the share of Gus Zook's money they thought was rightfully theirs. Whoever they were, they were in Johnstown in court today—just like her aunt and uncle. She was very close to the truth, and to her surprise that felt a little scary. What if Moriah was right, and there were some things a kid shouldn't know?

Speaking of Moriah, she was still the only kid her own age Effie had met in all of Pennsylvania. It was too bad they were having a fight. She would feel a lot less anxious if she had Moriah with her.

Maybe it wasn't that big a fight, she thought. *I've had bigger fights with Jasmine, and we're still friends. I could declare this an emergency, couldn't I? The worst she can do is ignore me.*

Effie got up from the table, rinsed her dishes, went to the coat closet by the front door, and rooted there till she found a scarf. It was plaid with only a little pink in it, but it would do. She tied it around her waist, went out the back door, and ran.

"Hi, Alfred," she said as she rushed by, "and Boris, you can go back to sleep."

Effie was a girl on a mission.

The field south of the house was about an acre

square. Mowed every few weeks to keep the weeds down, it was otherwise a collection of ruts, roots, and gopher holes. In the hot sun, it seemed to Effie it took forever before, sweaty and a little dizzy, she came into the shade of the woods. Through the trees, she could just make out the split-rail fence that marked the edge of the Yoders' property.

It wasn't hard to find the old hemlock, which rose above the oaks and maples. About two feet off the ground, a broken stub of a branch protruded from the trunk, giving Effie a first step. She put her right foot on it, reached for a branch above her, and started climbing.

Soon she was breathing hard and moving steadily. When the tree limbs thinned out, she stopped and admired the view. By then she was above the other trees, looking at Moriah's roof and below that at the highway. With her knees, she stabilized her body against the trunk, yanked the scarf from around her waist, waved it free, and tossed one end straight up till it caught a branch above her.

Then, fast but careful, she climbed down—hoping very hard that Moriah would look in the right direction soon.

To her surprise, Boris was on the ground waiting for her, his ears on high alert.

"Hey, Boris. Good dog. Thanks for looking out for me," Effie said.

Boris wagged his tail. Then the two of them walked out of the woods and back toward home together. They were almost across the field when Boris raised his head and Effie heard a voice. "Hey! Wait up!"

It was Moriah, with E.J. trailing behind.

Oh, thank goodness, Effie thought, and for a second she wanted to cry. It was good that she wasn't Effie on her own anymore. It was good to be part of a team.

Breathing hard, Moriah caught up. "What's the emergency?"

"Emergency?" E.J. repeated. "Cool! What kind?"

"The kind where we uncover clues," Effie said. "And Moriah, I'm sorry I—"

"I'm sorry, too," Moriah said. "Maybe you didn't mean to insult my pa?"

Grateful for an easy out, Effie said, "I didn't."

"Well, I didn't mean to pitch a hissy fit either," Moriah said.

E.J. made a sour face. "Girl stuff—*bleah!*" he said.

"Where are your folks? How come you could answer the signal so fast?" Effie asked.

"They had to go out of town today," Moriah said. "Something they were all excited about—I don't know what. They won't be back till late. Luke and Adam are in charge, but they don't care what we do."

"Moriah." Effie stopped in her tracks. "Your folks aren't down in Johnstown, are they?"

"Yeah, I think so. Johnstown," Moriah said. "How did you know?"

Effie didn't answer right away. Her mind had kicked into high gear. Aunt Clare and Uncle Ted were in Johnstown. That was where the mystery heirs had gone to court over her great-grandfather's estate. Did the Yoders have something to do with the court case? Could the Yoders be—?

"Come on!" E.J. tugged Effie's arm. "Are we gonna uncover clues now, or what?"

"Yes," said Effie. "Sure we are. Sorry." She started walking again, and while she walked she explained about the shed.

E.J. was one hundred percent enthusiastic at the prospect of entering forbidden territory.

Moriah was not. "If there's something your aunt and uncle don't want you to see, maybe you shouldn't see it," she said. "Maybe it's inappropriate for children. Grown-ups know best, Effie."

Effie did not want another fight. She wanted Moriah on her side. She spoke carefully. "In some families the grown-ups probably know best," Effie said, "but not necessarily in my family."

Meanwhile, E.J. was all over the word "inappropriate." "What if it's a *dead body?*" he aked.

Effie had to laugh. "I don't think so. My aunt and uncle don't even kill spiders."

"Aw, too bad," said E.J., "but let's go take a look."

27

The shed that had once been Gus Zook's workshop looked like an oversized shoe box with a pitched roof and a front porch. It was covered with ropy vines, living and dead. Its paint was faded and peeling.

Still tugging Effie's arm, E.J. said, "Come on. Let's do this, okay?"

"Why are you in such a hurry?" Effie asked. "Do you really think we're going to find a body?"

"Maybe," E.J. said, "and also Moriah promised me berry juice."

Effie stepped up onto the rickety porch and crossed it on tiptoes, avoiding holes and broken planks. Whatever creatures lived under there, she'd rather not pay them a visit feet-first. In three steps, she was trying to twist the rusty doorknob, but no go.

"Window?" Moriah said. "We could pry the boards loose with a crowbar."

Effie's heart sank. They'd have to get a crowbar from the garage. They'd have to get something to stand on. It would take a while. Her aunt and uncle wouldn't be gone forever. Annoyed, she grabbed the knob again and shook it, and what do you know? The knob came off in her hand.

"Take that, you old doorknob!" E.J. cried. "Oh boy, oh boy. Push hard, Effie! You might be wrong! There *might* be a body!"

The hinges squealed when Effie pushed, but the door opened wide—no teetering piles of junk in its way. Since the windows were blocked, the only light came from the doorway, but it was enough to reveal a sparsely furnished space.

A slanted table for drawing. A stool. Bookcases. A desk with a filing cabinet. A bulletin board. Framed pictures. Yellowed, spotted papers with crinkled edges tacked up here and there. A 1977 wall calendar open to August. The picture was a convertible sports car.

Except for dust and decay, the room was so well preserved it almost seemed that Gus Zook might come back any minute, and if he did, he would be gray and dust-covered too.

The girls were creeped out. E.J. was delighted. "Spooky!" he cried, and edged by them. "What are you waiting for? Let's look around!"

All that little-kid energy broke the spell. Effie and Moriah breathed again, embarrassed to have hesitated. By the time they stepped inside, E.J. was already opening drawers.

"Awww, it's *boring*!" he said. "Pens and rulers and . . . what's this thing?"

"A protractor," said Effie, "for measuring angles."

"And what's this?" E.J. held up a squat little bottle he had found on the table.

"For ink," said Moriah.

"Cool," said E.J., but he had already moved on.

The lights didn't work, and it was hard to see. Effie used her phone as a flashlight to study drawings on the wall behind the slanted table.

"The lost plans," she murmured, "the gap in the record. It's here."

"What?" Moriah asked.

"These look like plans for new inventions," Effie said out loud. It was hard to make sense of the diagrams, especially in the poor light, but she could read the titles, all of them written in her great-grandfather's small, neat print: *Steam-Powered Jet Engine, Bicycle Seat Belt, Automobile Umbrella, Dogs' Ear Cuff.*

"Wait—what's the last one?" Moriah looked over Effie's shoulder at a drawing of a dog eating from a dish, his floppy ears squished under a band around his head and neck.

"It doesn't look comfortable," Moriah said.

"If I was a dog wearing that, I'd be embarrassed," said E.J. "It's dumb."

"It is not!" Effie leaped to her great-grandfather's defense. "It's clever. The band keeps the dog's ears out of his food, so they don't get dirty. That's good, right?"

Moriah looked at the next drawing. "A seat belt for a bike wouldn't keep you safe," she said. "It would only guarantee that you and the bike crashed together."

"All these ideas are dumb," said E.J.

"Hey—you take that back!" said Effie. "You guys are insulting my . . . Oh." Effie stopped, realizing she was defending her great-grandfather the same way Moriah had defended her father the day before. Effie had never met Gus Zook, but she still felt family loyalty.

Moriah must have understood. "Sorry, Effie," she said.

"No." Effie took a breath. "You guys are right. They *are* bad ideas. But you know what else? I feel sad for my great-grandfather. He was out here all by himself in his workshop, trying to come up with something good—as good as a barf bag. But the best he could do was a headband for dogs."

There were more papers on the wall, not plans but phrases written in fancy letters, calligraphy. Effie trained her flashlight on a few:

The parent teaches the child to know lovable from despicable.

Fate cares more about your wrongs than your rights.

A man's beard signifies his special place in the natural order.

"I know those. They're precepts!" E.J. said.

"So you were right after all, Effie," said Moriah. "Your great-grandfather must've inspired BFA, some of it at least. But it was my pa's idea to call them precepts. Did you read the last part of Gus Zook's story at the museum?"

Effie nodded. "Just today."

"Do you remember it says something about a civilization 'united, hygienic, and content'? I recognized that. It's a precept too," Moriah said.

E.J.'s thumb had been in his mouth. Now he removed it. "Number twenty-three."

Effie looked down at E.J. "How old are you again?"

"Four, but I'm short for my age," said E.J.

"Also smart," said Effie.

"I know it," said E.J., and he replaced his thumb in his mouth.

The sun had sunk by this time and shone through the open doorway. Effie looked at her phone—4:05. For all she knew, her aunt and uncle were home by now. "We should go," she said. "We can come back, but we can't tell anyone."

"You promised berry juice," E.J. reminded his sister.

"I know I did, E.J. I—," she started to say, but she was rudely interrupted by a tremendous noise—part crunch, part crash, it made the rickety building shake.

"Wh-wh-what was—," E.J. stammered, but his voice was drowned out by a succession of thumps overhead, and then a high-pitched, unhappy *ble-e-e-eat*, followed by Boris, right outside, barking up a storm.

"Goat on the roof," Moriah said calmly.

"*What?*" Effie said.

"Watch out!" Moriah said, no longer calm, as—*crack*—the ceiling splintered, then—*pat-patter-pat*—pieces of wood and tar paper rained down on the floor.

After that, a leg came through, a big black one with a hoof on the end that proceeded to dangle and kick hopelessly while Effie, Moriah, and E.J. dodged, making every shrill, freaked-out sound a person threatened by a goat leg can make.

Effie said, "Alfred!" as if the mean black goat was falling through the ceiling on purpose. Then more bits and pieces came down, followed by a second leg, then two more legs, a tail, and the rest of Alfred too.

When the goat hit the floor, the shed shook again and a framed photograph fell from its place on the wall. Helpless against the general destruction, Effie at least managed to save that.

While Boris barked, E.J. yelled, and Moriah insisted, "Let's get out of here!" Effie looked at the photograph in her hand. It showed a woman wearing a skirt and jacket. She had a hat on her head and a smile on her face. She looked sophisticated and happy. She was black.

Effie took all this in at a glance, but it was the inscription that made her heart go *thud*. She had thought no more surprises were possible that day, but she had been wrong.

And there was one more surprise to come.

None of the kids heard the grown-ups calling from outside till one of them appeared in the doorway. Backlit by the sun, her blond hair formed a halo. Effie looked up and feared for a split second that the vision was an angel.

It wasn't, though. It was her mother, live and in the flesh.

CHAPTER
28

Poor Alfred.

For a long time, he had wanted to break the latch on his gate and make a run for it. That afternoon he had finally succeeded. He could have gone anywhere, but where he went was the end of the driveway. The shed there had looked sturdy enough, its roof a perfect place from which to survey his expanded domain.

What Alfred didn't know was how many summers and winters that roof had endured. It was plumb worn out, not sturdy anymore, and its collapse was such a shock that Alfred underwent a transformation. From that moment on, he ceased to be irascible, ornery, and aggressive and became instead docile, affable, and retiring.

The humans didn't catch on right away, but Boris did and nipped at Alfred's heels, herding him out the door, off the porch, and back in the direction of his pen.

Everybody else, meanwhile, was hugging and crying. In fact, there was such an abundance of gladness that it splashed over to E.J. and Moriah, who were invited for hors d'oeuvres on the front porch. For the time being, it didn't matter that they were Yoders. Everyone was welcome.

"I don't mean to be a pill," E.J. said as they all walked down the driveway toward the yellow farmhouse, "but Moriah did promise me berry juice."

"What?" Effie looked down to see that E.J. was gripping her hand. She hadn't even noticed. Her heart was full at the same time her mind was working fast. Johnstown. The precepts. The inscription on the photo. Even her own good throwing arm—and Moriah's and Mr. Odbody's too.

If she was right, she was finally face-to-face with the truth.

And it was unbelievable.

"Berry juice?" E.J. repeated. "Hello-o-o?"

"Sadie," Effie said, "Mr. Odbody's grandmother."

E.J. frowned and dropped Effie's hand. "Never mind. I'll get berry juice from someone else."

It took a while for the chairs on the porch to be dusted off and shifted, for people to sit down, for Uncle Ted to slice cheese, get out crackers and olives, plate the raw vegetables, and locate the extra napkins in the pantry. Meanwhile, Aunt Clare made drinks, which Moriah helped distribute. There were plenty of cherries. E.J. got one in his berry juice.

When at last everyone had settled and had a chance to breathe, Effie's mother spoke. "I suppose you're wondering how I got back so fast from the Pacific."

Effie said, "Not really." For her, it was enough that her mom was there. The details could wait.

Molly Zook looked surprised and a little disappointed.

"I'm wondering," Moriah said politely.

"The US Air Force," said Effie's mom. "Specifically, Air Mobility Command. The joke is that AMC means 'airplane maybe come,' but I got lucky. I had to fly commercial from St. Louis, but the connections were good. There was only one seat, so Effie's dad—Mr. Starr, I mean—stayed behind to do some mop-up."

"That's very interesting," Moriah said politely.

"*I* thought so," said Molly. "Would you like to hear about how I was rescued? Sharks were involved. Effie?"

"I want to hear all about it, Mom," Effie said. "But not right now. Right now I have some questions."

"Oh dear," said Aunt Clare.

"Are you okay, Effie?" said her mom. "You seem distracted. Whose photo is that? Did it come from the workshop?"

"The shed," Aunt Clare corrected her.

"It is not a shed," said Effie. "It was never a shed. It was Gus Zook's workshop. And you and Uncle Ted closed it up because you didn't want anybody to know how dumb his last inventions were."

"Oh dear," said Aunt Clare.

Uncle Ted sighed. "Your great-grandmother wanted to protect Gus Zook's reputation, Effie. She locked up the shed after Gus Zook died. Till you came, we had half forgotten it was there. But with all the, uh . . . controversy lately, it seemed like a bad idea for you to be poking around."

Moriah shifted uncomfortably in her chair, pushed it back, and stood up. "Come on, E.J. We should go. Thanks, everybody, for the—"

"No, Moriah, you *shouldn't* go," said Effie. "Please stay. We're all family, after all. Right, Mom? Right, Aunt Clare?"

"Oh dear," said Aunt Clare.

"Clare? If you say 'oh dear' one more time, I will scream," said Effie's mom.

"My sentiments exactly," said Uncle Ted.

"Well, what do you want me to say?" said Aunt Clare.

"The truth would be good," Effie said. "I will start. Moriah, your parents went to Johnstown to a court hearing today. They were there because your dad was trying to claim his part of Gus Zook's estate. He is Gus Zook's grandchild, just like my mom and Aunt Clare are. And you and E.J. are his great-grandchildren, just like me."

"I'm a Zook?" E.J. scratched his head. "I thought I was a Yoder."

"You're a Zook and a Yoder both," said Effie. "And if you don't want to faint from surprise, you better take some deep breaths, because that is only the start."

Effie held up the photo she had rescued from the workshop and read the inscription out loud: "'For Gus, All my love in spite of everything, Sadie.'"

E.J. made a face. "Mushy stuff—*bleah*."

Moriah sat back down. "It makes sense," she said slowly. "Our grandma—my dad's mom—is biracial. It doesn't come up because she pretty much looks white, but it's not a secret. Once I asked her to tell me about when she was little, and she said she didn't like to talk about it. But I know she had a brother. After she got married, she didn't see him or her mother, either."

"And she was from Johnstown, right?" said Effie.

"She was," said Moriah.

Aunt Clare sighed and shook her head. "Now that the judge has decided, that reporter from Harrisburg will put it all in the paper tomorrow. Do you want to explain, Molly? Or shall I?"

"You're doing fine," said Effie's mom.

Aunt Clare took a breath as if her speech would be a long one. "Moriah's grandmother was born at the county hospital along with a twin brother. Their mother was Sadie Pendleton, and their father—as you know by now—was Gus Zook.

"For a while, Sadie and the twins stayed on their family farm—the one next door where the Yoders live now. In effect, they were Gus's second family. I guess he tried to keep them a secret."

Effie remembered how people in Penn Creek knew all about her even before she met them. "How do you keep such a big secret in such a small town?" she asked.

"Exactly," said her mother. "He didn't."

"Your great-grandmother must have known," Aunt Clare said. "And before the twins were very big, Sadie sold her land and moved away. If I had to bet, I'd say Effie the First laid down the law to Gus: Either they go, or I do. As far as I know, they never came back, and Gus never saw the children again."

"That's terrible," said Moriah.

Aunt Clare shrugged. "It is, but it was a long time

ago and attitudes were different. My grandmother wanted to keep her family together and protect her son from the scandal. Once the evidence was out of the way, they tried to pretend nothing had ever happened."

"There's something else, too," said Effie's mom. "Sadie was mixed-race. You will have noticed there aren't a lot of African-Americans in this neck of the woods even now. There is still a lot of prejudice, and there was more back then. It can't have been comfortable for her around here."

"It wasn't right for Gus Zook to lie to his wife, to Effie the First," Effie said.

"Even great men aren't perfect," said Uncle Ted.

E.J.'s eyes were as big as quarters. "This is better than cartoons."

Moriah said, "It's grown-up stuff. You shouldn't be listening."

"Hold your breath, E.J., and you'll forget," said Effie.

"Why would I want to do that?" E.J. asked.

"Hang on a sec," said Moriah, and Effie could almost see her calculating. "My grandmother and her brother are the twins you're talking about. They're Sadie's children, and Mr. Odbody's grandmother is the same Sadie, so that means—"

Effie nodded. "Like I said, the story gets better. Mr. Odbody is your cousin—my half-cousin, if there is such a thing. And he went with your parents to Johnstown today to claim a share of Gus Zook's estate."

CHAPTER

29

E.J. wanted to know what an estate was. And then he wanted to know if now his family was rich, because if they were, he wanted a fridge in his room with bottles and bottles of berry juice.

Before E.J.'s questions were answered, Moriah asked Effie or someone to explain one more time exactly how all the family relations worked.

Effie's mom said she'd give it a try. "When Sadie's twins grew up, the boy married a black woman. Their son is the man you know as Pendleton Odbody. The girl—Patricia—married a white man, Stanley Yoder."

"Hey, that's our grandma and grandpa!" E.J. said.

"And their son, Rob, is your dad," Aunt Clare said.

"Since they are from Johnstown—and Sadie lived there too—that's the court where they filed their claim."

"You told me 'Odbody' isn't his real name," Effie reminded her aunt.

"Because it's not," Aunt Clare said. "A couple of years ago he came back to town, found the building where the bookstore is, and rented it from us. We didn't know who he was, and he didn't want us to. So he used an assumed name."

"Funny name," said E.J.

"How did he and Mr. Yoder find each other?" Effie asked.

"It's all in the court papers," Uncle Ted said. "Both of them were trying to buy the farm their grand-mother had once owned. Mr. Yoder was the high bidder, but during the negotiations they realized they were related."

"Did Mr. Yoder know then that he was Gus Zook's grandchild—that they both were?" Effie asked.

"The court filing says he got interested in Gus Zook's ideas first," Aunt Clare said. "In the museum's archive he found a letter Sadie had written to Gus and asked his mother about it. As Moriah says, she didn't want anything to do with her past. I think that's why she never tried to make a claim on the estate herself."

Effie looked at Moriah. "It's only fair that your family gets half our money."

"What?" Aunt Clare squeaked. "After all this time? And it wouldn't be *half* our money, Effie. After we paid back all those years of the income from the patent, it would be almost all of it."

"That can't be helped," said Effie. "Moriah's family is just as much Gus Zook's relatives as we are."

"Thank you," said Moriah.

"You're welcome," said Effie.

"Maybe we should have told you the truth sooner, Effie," Aunt Clare said. "But I didn't think it was right that a child should have to deal with family drama."

"We don't know much about children," Effie's uncle put in.

"It wasn't right to hide the truth either," Effie said. "Is the lawsuit why you were so worried all the time, why you were too busy to keep track of me?"

"Wait—too busy to keep track of her, *what*?" Effie's mother looked from Clare to Ted.

They looked sheepish.

Effie piped up. "I was fine on my own, Mom. I got really good at bike riding, and Mr. Odbody's one of my best friends. At least he was. Also, we had hors d'oeuvres in the parlor every night."

"We did do that," said Uncle Ted hopefully.

"We will talk later," said Effie's mom.

Aunt Clare explained. "We thought we would need the money from selling property to pay the claim after the judge made his decision. That's why we canceled Mr. Odbody's lease, too, so we could sell that building."

"You didn't have to cancel it in such a hurry," Effie said.

"Maybe not," Aunt Clare admitted. "But we didn't like it when we learned you were spending so much time there."

"Speak for yourself," said Uncle Ted.

"Mr. Odbody was suing us, suing your own family," Aunt Clare defended herself. "I phoned him as soon as we got home from Fourthfest. I told him that under the circumstances, he was not suitable company for my niece. I guess our words got heated, and he posted the closed sign right away."

"If Mr. Odbody's not suitable company for Effie, then E.J. and I aren't either," Moriah said. "There's still bad blood between our families."

Aunt Clare looked like she wanted to argue but couldn't find the words. Uncle Ted looked sad, which was the way Effie felt. She had just gained a cousin. Was she about to lose her?

"There doesn't have to be bad blood," Effie said. "How about if Moriah and E.J. stay for dinner, and we can call Mr. Odbody, too, and also Mr. and Mrs. Yoder. All we have to decide is what to eat. Shall we order pizza? Alternatively, we could order pizza. Oh wait, unless now we're too broke for takeout?"

"We're not too broke," said Uncle Ted.

"The judge ruled in our favor," said Aunt Clare.

"We won?" said Effie.

"We lost?" said Moriah.

"Mr. Yoder and Mr. Odbody waited too long," said Uncle Ted. "The law says a will can't be overturned more than ten years after the estate's settled."

"So we're still well fixed," said Effie.

"Actually," said Effie's mom, "we're rich."

CHAPTER

30

Effie was a tiny bit disappointed. She had just been getting used to being poor. She was imagining herself as a stout-hearted waif dressed in rags, with Moriah, the kind princess wearing overalls and a Steelers cap, offering her toys and canned goods and blankets.

"I'm sorry, Moriah," said Effie.

"That's okay," Moriah said. "I wouldn't know how to be rich anyway."

"Can we get pepperoni on the pizza?" E.J. asked.

Moriah shook her head and stood up for the second time. "We can't stay. Pa and Mama must be home by now. We better make tracks or they'll worry. Maybe we can come over another time."

"Is Pa gonna skin us?" E.J. stood up too.

"You can count on reciting a few dozen precepts," Moriah said.

"Are we going to tell him we've been to Zooks'?" E.J. asked.

"We're going to tell him we've been with our cousins," said Moriah.

"Even if there's precepts, it was worth it," E.J. said. "I got berry juice. And I got to hear a story."

Once Moriah and E.J. had left for home, Uncle Ted took in the hors d'oeuvres plates. When he came back, Chop Suey was right behind him, his tail waving as proudly as a flag. Effie grabbed for him, but the cat jumped up into Aunt Clare's lap, circled, and made himself comfortable.

Frowning, Aunt Clare leaned back in her chair. "Where did *he* come from?" she asked.

"He belongs to Mr. Odbody," Effie said. "He lives at the bookstore—well, *lived* at the bookstore, back when there was a bookstore."

"He can't stay here," Aunt Clare said. "I hate cats."

"I see that," said Effie.

"She always has," said Effie's mom.

"There's a simple solution," said Uncle Ted. "We could reinstate Mr. Odbody's lease and let him reopen Sadie's."

Aunt Clare opened her mouth to say, "Oh dear" but at the last second changed it to "Fine." Then she added, "Would someone please remove this cat from my person?"

Effie was happy to do so.

The sun crept toward the horizon. There were no clouds in the sky to turn color and make day's end beautiful, but Effie could look forward to the fireflies. Uncle Ted had just called to order the pizza when a rattletrap car turned into the driveway from the road below, climbed the hill slowly, and stopped between the house and the garage.

As Effie and her family watched, a thin young woman with stringy hair got out. A notebook was in her left hand. A pen was clenched between her teeth. Her expression was determined.

"Uh-oh—the press," said Uncle Ted. "Shall I call Mrs. McMinty?"

"I think we can handle her," said Effie's mom.

The woman strode toward the house and climbed the porch steps. She opened her notebook, took the pen in her right hand, and said, "I just have a few questions."

"Go away," said Aunt Clare.

"Oh, cut her some slack," said Effie's mom. "What will it hurt to offer up the family's point of view? We're grateful that the wheels of justice . . . yada, yada . . . time to heal, and so forth."

"Care for a ginger ale?" Uncle Ted asked the woman.

"Thanks, but I'm on deadline," she said. "I have to get back to Harrisburg."

"Oh, wow, you must be Tapper Sprocket!" said Effie.

The young woman was obviously surprised. "I am, yeah," she said. "You must be Effie, right?"

"Effie Starr Zook," Effie said. "Two *r*'s in 'Starr.'"

Tapper said, "Nice to meet you. Uh"—she looked to the grown-ups—"like I said, I have a few questions."

"*That* sounds like someone I know," said Effie's mom.

The young reporter looked at Molly as though she couldn't place her. Then she did, and her eyebrows shot skyward. "How did you get here so fast?" she asked. "Is it true you were almost devoured by sharks?"

"Imagine that. Someone cares," said Molly.

"Miss Sprocket," Effie said, "can I ask you something? Do you get paid to ask questions?"

Tapper Sprocket smiled. Her skin was sallow, but her smile was beautiful. "I do, yeah," she said. "Not much, but I do."

Effie sighed. "How wonderful is that? If I could get paid to ask questions, being a grown-up might be okay."

31

Once Tapper Sprocket's story appeared in the paper, other media picked it up, and for a few days no one in America could turn on the TV or stand in line at the supermarket without seeing the faces of Yoders and Zooks before them.

In some versions of the story, the Yoders were the bad guys, trying to take the Zooks' money and destroy a great man's reputation. In others, the Zooks were the villains, greedily hogging money that should never have been theirs and defending a man who wasn't that great after all.

This was all very hard on the real Yoders and Zooks, but, unexpectedly, shared suffering brought them together, same as during war or natural disaster. In the end—either to make themselves look good, or genuinely to be nice—Effie's family agreed to share half of all future barf bag proceeds with Rob Yoder and Pendleton Odbody. It wasn't as much money as the lawsuit had asked for, but it wasn't chicken feed, either.

When Rob and Pendleton agreed, the bad blood between the families came to an end. To celebrate, Mr. Odbody invited all his cousins, Mrs. McMinty, and Mr. Barnes to Sadie's Books for a reception.

Effie's parents couldn't make it. Since they weren't broke after all, they were back in Hawaii, overseeing the raising of *Sunspot I* from the bottom of the ocean.

Luke and Adam Yoder were also absent. It was mid-August by this time, and they had football practice.

The rest of the guests all showed up, and they dressed nicely too. Effie wore a sleeveless sheath dress that had arrived FedEx from Bergdorf's. Mr. Barnes, now clean-shaven, and Mr. Odbody were both wearing sports coats. Moriah had abandoned her usual overalls in favor of a red sundress with matching Converse low-tops. Mrs. McMinty's shorts were less baggy than usual, but the real surprise was her T-shirt, which read MAUREEN MCMINTY FOR MAYOR.

"I hope you don't mind having some competition," she told Rob Yoder. "I'm looking forward to lively debates. Perhaps we can address BFA Precept Two, 'the special place of women in the natural order of things'?"

Mr. Yoder being momentarily speechless, his wife stepped in. "I'll look forward to those debates myself," Anjelica Yoder said. "Had you heard, Maureen, that Pendleton has offered me a job? With his new income, he can afford some help around the store, and I've always loved to read."

Effie and Moriah were together pouring drinks at the counter.

"So are you coming to visit over Labor Day or not?" Effie asked her.

"Still not sure," Moriah said.

"What's the problem?" Effie said. "My friends are nice. Don't you want to see the Statue of Liberty? And eat ten kinds of wood-fired pizza?"

"I don't have the right clothes," Moriah said. "I can't exactly wear overalls, can I?"

"In Brooklyn, lots of people do," said Effie.

"What about your friends?" Moriah asked.

"They don't wear overalls," Effie admitted. "Remember when I thought you were a boy?"

"Sure," said Moriah. "In my family, it's easier to be a boy. Besides, overalls are what you wear to work outdoors."

"So when you come," Effie said, "we'll go shopping. My family's rich remember? I can be the benevolent fairy princess, and—"

Moriah giggled. "Cut it out, Effie. My family's not rich, but I can afford to buy clothes. Wouldn't the kids at my school be surprised if I showed up in designer jeans?"

"Exactly!" said Effie. "You have to come."

"Maybe," said Moriah.

Effie had been right to think that she and Moriah were different. But she'd been wrong to think that was bad. In fact, it just gave them more to talk about.

Mr. Barnes came up. "I brought that postcard you asked for, Effie," he said, removing it from an inside pocket. "That will be twenty-five cents. I'd like to give it to you for nothing, but we lost out on some funding when Moriah's pa's lawsuit didn't go as expected."

"I've got money." Effie went for her purse and came back with a quarter, her aunt's copy of *Pippi Longstocking*, and two questions. "Mr. Barnes, did you join BFA because you wanted a big donation from Mr. Yoder? Is he the one who suggested the men's grooming exhibit, too?"

Mr. Barnes said, "Of course not," but his face had turned pink.

"So I guess you didn't shave because you lost the donation?" Effie said.

"I shaved because I itched," said Mr. Barnes.

Moriah leaned over to look at the postcard. It was the one with a photo of the original sketch for the barf bag. "Why did you want that?" she asked.

"You'll see," Effie said. She opened *Pippi Longstocking* to the flyleaf, then looked from it to the postcard and nodded. "Thought so," she said. "Everybody?" She clinked a spoon against a glass to get their attention. "I have something to say. Can you hear me all right?"

E.J. removed his thumb from his mouth. "Sure!"

"Okay, then." Effie cleared her throat and looked

into the far distance. "Here goes. I believe that the barf bag was actually invented by Effie Zook, Effie the First, that is."

Effie had never actually heard stunned silence before, much less been the cause of it. She found the sensation pleasant. Aunt Clare spoke first. "Honey, that is nonsense. Gus Zook was a great man."

"You know what, Aunt Clare? Some things aren't true, no matter how many times you say them."

"I don't get it," said Moriah. "How do you know?"

Effie held up *Pippi Longstocking*.

"That's mine," said Aunt Clare. "I loved it as a kid."

"Your grandmother wrote you a note inside. See?" Effie displayed the flyleaf for inspection. Next, she held up the postcard. "Notice anything?"

"Same loopy handwriting," Aunt Clare said in a quiet voice. "But that doesn't prove—"

"Not prove," Effie admitted. "But Effie the First went to college too. Why wouldn't she have been as smart as her husband? Or smarter? Maybe she was tired of being barfed on every time she and Gus got in an airplane. The barf bag was her solution."

"Barfed on!" E.J. cracked up.

Uncle Ted, meanwhile, was nodding. "Different times back then. Gus Zook might've thought the patent office and manufacturers would take a man's idea more seriously. He might've convinced Effie that was the case too."

"She could have said something later," said Aunt Clare.

"Maybe she didn't think anyone would believe her," said Mr. Odbody.

"If that's it, she might have been right," said Mrs. McMinty. "Everyone in this town thought Gus Zook was the great man, and she the kind and dutiful wife. In general, people don't like to change their minds. It's too much work."

"What do you think, Rob?" Mrs. Yoder turned to her husband. "You know Zookiana better than anybody."

"I think I should've noticed the handwriting myself," he said. "Maybe I didn't want to. But I still believe Gus Zook was a great man and a great thinker."

"I'm not saying he wasn't," Effie said. "All I'm saying is he didn't invent the barf bag."

No one replied to that, but Effie didn't care. She had made her point. It had taken her most of the summer, but she had asked a lot of questions and learned a little truth. Next time she studied her great-grandmother's face in the silver frame, she would understand her better.

What Effie thought was, *Effie Zook was a great woman.*

What she said was, "Who wants a glass of ginger ale? We've got plenty of cherries."

AUTHOR'S NOTE

The real inventor of the emesis bag was not from Central Pennsylvania but from North Dakota. His name was Gilmore Schjeldahl, and unlike Gus Zook's, his subsequent engineering innovations were also successful. Besides devising innovations that protected research balloons, satellites, and Polaris missiles, he helped refine a medical device that clears diseased arteries around the heart. Schjeldahl died in 2002.

I didn't learn about Mr. Schjeldahl until after I finished drafting the book, and I am glad to be able to give the inventor his due here.

Like most books, this one results from several inspirations meeting and mixing it up in the author's head.

First off was a girl I met at a reading in rural Pennsylvania. Her name was Moriah, a fact she had to whisper in my ear for fear her parents might find out she had told a stranger. I never learned more, but that vignette stayed with me, and from it Rob Yoder and Beards for America were born.

The real Effie Zook (she spelled it Zuck) was a

wonderful friend and artist who made the most glorious year-round wreaths from greenery and wildflowers. She wasn't well fixed, at least not as far as I know, but she was abundantly rich in spirit. She died in 2012, and her daughter Leslie and I remain friends. My own daughter, Rosa, spent a summer volunteering on Leslie's Pennsylvania farm—so there you have further inspiration.

I needed a heroic project for Effie's parents and as sometimes happens, the universe handed me a gift in the form of *Solar Impulse*, the real-life round-the world flight of a sun-powered airplane—still in progress at the time of this writing. Happily, *Solar Impulse* never had to ditch in the Pacific, but its flight path and tribulations provided credible fodder for my story.

Another real-life inspiration was my friend Sharif, whom I borrowed to play the part of Pendleton Odbody. An African American bookstore proprietor in a small Central Pennsylvania town might be forgiven for seeing himself as an odd body. If anyone could carry off the role with aplomb, I knew it was Sharif.

Research for other projects got me thinking about

the artificiality of the lines between races. See, for example, the 44th president who is as white as he is black (just ask his Kansas cousins), or the descendants of Sally Hemings and the third president, Thomas Jefferson. My own overwhelmingly Caucasian family tree is graced by a Native American woman. My friend Sharif's mother, who is black, remembers as a child having to use the back door to enter the home of a mixed-race aunt who "passed" as white.

The truth is we are all descended from the first humans in Africa 100,000 years ago. Subsequent divisions by race, ethnicity, tribe, you-name-it have never been anything but destructive. In the book, Effie's dauntless questioning reveals unexpected truths—and unexpected relatives—and our open-minded hero takes the truths in her stride and embraces the cousins. Most members of her community do the same. Unfortunately it's possible that even in the 21st century, the nonfiction reaction might be different.

The alchemical reactions that yield a book develop over time. This one had been drafted and revised before I realized I was retelling the story of Isaac and Ishmael from *Genesis*, with one important difference:

centuries of strife nipped in the bud, happy ending achieved. Well, why not? As Dr. Seuss wrote in *Horton Hatches the Egg,* my favorite of all his books, "It should be, it should be, it should be like that."